*Where the Heart Waits*

**Other Avalon Books by Charlene Bowen**

*A SUMMER'S LOVE DREAM*
*REACH FOR A STAR*
*TO CATCH A RAINBOW*
*THE WANDERING HEART*

# Where the HEART WAITS

CHARLENE BOWEN

*AVALON BOOKS*
THOMAS BOUREGY AND COMPANY, INC.
401 LAFAYETTE STREET
NEW YORK, NEW YORK 10003

Library of Congress Catalog Card Number: 91-92221
ISBN 0-8034-8894-7


PRINTED IN THE UNITED STATES OF AMERICA
ON ACID-FREE PAPER
BY HADDON CRAFTSMEN, SCRANTON, PENNSYLVANIA

To Sally, with love

# *Chapter One*

Serena Cole felt distinctly out of place as she surveyed the other occupants of the small southwestern Idaho airport terminal. Denim jeans and casual cotton dresses seemed to be the order of the day. She felt that her trim blue-linen suit, which had somehow managed to retain its fresh, unwrinkled appearance during the long flight from Boston's Logan Airport, stood out like that proverbial sore thumb.

The terminal was taking on a deserted air as the other passengers who had arrived on her flight collected their luggage and departed. She scanned the rapidly thinning crowd, looking for—she wasn't sure whom. Although the letter in her purse said she would be met by Farley, one of the hands from the Double C, who would drive her out to the ranch, she had no idea how she was to recognize this Farley. It was fairly obvious, however, that there was nobody around who was looking for her.

The only person who seemed to be paying any attention to her at all was a tall, lean man who had been conducting some business at a counter with a sign over it that read, *Ramp Service*. Ever since she had entered the terminal, she'd had the feeling he was watching her disapprovingly. She wondered what she could possibly have done to offend him, since she'd never seen him before in her life. Was it her attire, perhaps, or her obvious air of not being from around here?

She was aware that everything about her identified her as a "city girl," and an Easterner at that. Maybe he was just one of those independent Western types she'd heard about who disliked outsiders, who felt they should stay in the city where they belonged. The thought sent a flash of anger through her. Drawing herself up to her full five feet three inches, she met his gaze levelly, determined to show him that he couldn't intimidate her with his forbidding looks and his air of superiority.

He frowned slightly when he saw that she was looking back at him. Serena's first impulse was to lower her eyes under that stern, uncompromising stare, but she forced herself to face up to him. She noted, with satisfaction, that he looked away first.

She realized the terminal was nearly empty now. What if nobody had come for her by the time everyone else had gone? She had a sudden vision of being the only one left in the airport, like a piece of forgotten luggage.

Giving herself a mental shake, she told herself to stop being ridiculous. She was a competent, intelligent young woman, supposedly capable of figuring out her next move. Surely there had to be a way of getting out to the Double C Ranch.

''Would Serena Cole please come to the Information counter?'' The sound of her own name being called over the public-address system, in a casual, folksy drawl, took her by surprise. She located the Information counter and identified herself.

''Y'got a phone call.'' The man behind the counter nodded toward the telephone.

''Serena Cole,'' she said into the mouthpiece, hoping the call had something to do with her missing ride.

It did. ''Miz Cole, this's Farley,'' a gravelly voice came over the line. ''Ma'am, I'm sure sorry I didn't get there to pick you up, but there wasn't nothing I could do about it. I spent the last couple of hours trying to get this danged pickup truck running.''

''But you'll be on your way soon, won't you?'' she asked in a hopeful tone.

''Wal, ma'am, I'm afraid not. I'm still working on it. I'll get there as soon as I can. Maybe if Homer gets back with the Jeep, one of us can run in and get you, but he's out riding fence, and there ain't no telling when . . .'' His voice trailed off, as if to indicate that this was not something she ought to count on.

Farley sounded apologetic, as well as just plain tired, and Serena wondered if her arrival was causing a great deal of trouble for him as well as for Homer. She knew from her correspondence with Ralph Hubbard, the local attorney who was settling her father's affairs, that Homer McCall was the other hand at the Double C. He and Farley had stayed on to look after things until some decision was made about the ranch. She had the uneasy feeling that perhaps she should have just stayed in Windham, the comfortable little town a few miles outside Boston where she'd lived all her life. It seemed that all she was accomplishing by insisting on coming out here was to disrupt other people's routines.

"Thanks for letting me know," she said. "I'll see if I can find some other way to get there."

After hanging up, she turned back to the man at the Information counter. "Is there any way I can get out to the Double C Ranch? A bus or a taxi or something?"

He shook his head with regret. " 'Fraid not. Your best bet would be to catch a ride with someone who's headed in that direction. Mitch Tanner is going out that way. He should be leaving any minute."

As much as Serena disliked the idea of begging favors from complete strangers, it seemed she had no choice. "How do I find this Mr. Tanner?" she asked.

"He's right over there. I'll talk to him for you if you'd like," he offered obligingly.

She turned her head in the direction of his glance and found herself looking at the tall man she'd noticed earlier. If this was Mitch Tanner, she had no intention of riding to the Double C or anywhere else with him. "Never mind, I'll find some other way—" she began.

But before she could finish the sentence, the man at the Information counter called out, "Hey, Mitch, can you come here for a minute?"

"Sure, Emmett," he replied in an amiable tone. As he took his time sauntering toward them, Serena had ample opportunity to study him. She wasn't sure what it was about the man that made him so noticeable. He appeared to be in his early to mid-thirties. He couldn't really be called handsome—at least not in the classic sense of the word. His face, with its high cheekbones, bushy eyebrows, and hawklike nose, was too angular and stark for that. Still, there was something arresting about those dark eyes and that shock of thick, almost black hair.

His attire was no different from that of the other men she'd seen in the terminal. His snap-buttoned shirt and the bandanna knotted at his throat were nondescript. Likewise, there was nothing distinguishing about the faded, much-washed jeans that hung loose and comfortable on his lean frame. The dusty boots that showed beneath the frayed hems of those jeans were similar to the ones worn by most of the other men in the vicinity.

Yet there was an indefinable something that set him apart. He seemed almost to be an aristocrat in disguise, who would be recognized—by his air of authority—even if he'd been dressed in beggar's clothes.

She pushed the thought out of her mind and scolded herself for being fanciful. *You've been watching too many old movies,* she told herself.

"Here's your chance to help a lady in distress," the man named Emmett said, nodding toward Serena. "Miss Cole needs a ride out to the Double C."

Mitch Tanner turned his attention to Serena, taking in every detail of her appearance. As she always did in moments of stress or uncertainty, Serena squared her slender shoulders, tilted her delicate chin at a determined angle, and retreated behind a facade of cool reserve.

She had been aptly named. The illusion of quiet composure was heightened by her serious blue eyes, whose color could change from light azure to a deep, smoky shade, depending on her mood. Her curtain of pale, shimmery, flaxen hair added to her air of poised, unruffled serenity.

When Mitch finished his scrutiny, he gave a curt nod, which could have denoted anything from approval over her looks to a grudging agreement to provide the transportation she needed. "We'd better get going," he said in a businesslike tone. "I want to get there before dark. These yours?" He indicated the two suitcases at her feet.

At her nod he picked up the larger bag and started to reach for the other one, but Serena made a quick grab for it. As her fingers closed around the handle, a fraction of a second before his, he gave a little shrug, as if to say, *Suit yourself.* She was relieved that he wasn't going to make an issue of the matter. Although she didn't want to be any more trouble to him than was absolutely necessary, neither did she care to engage in a tug-of-war over her luggage right here in the terminal.

She was surprised when he ushered her out the same door she'd come in earlier, the one that led out toward the runway. She'd thought the parking lot would be in the other direction. She was going to mention this but changed her mind after a glance at his impassive countenance. His manner discouraged questions. She had to almost run to keep up with his long-limbed stride as he led her past a hangar and a couple of other buildings.

"Here we are," he said, stopping in front of a neat red-and-silver airplane parked on a strip of blacktop. Block letters along its nose identified it as a Cherokee.

Serena looked from the small craft to Mitch, then back to the airplane. "You mean, we're going to *fly* out to the ranch?"

"That's the idea. You're not afraid, are you?"

"No, it's not that. I'm just—surprised." The four-seater *did* look awfully small, compared to the 737 that had brought her from Boston to Boise, or even the twin engine Beech Baron in which she'd completed the final leg of her trip. Yet nothing would have induced her to admit to even a slight trepidation. She realized he was watching her closely.

"You said you wanted to get there before dark," she reminded him. "Hadn't we better get started?"

Once she was securely buckled in, with her bags stowed in the luggage compartment, she relaxed somewhat. Despite its small size, the airplane looked substantial enough. Besides, although Mitch's calm, self-assured manner bordered on arrogance, his strong, capable hands on the controls left no doubt of his ability to handle the small craft.

Mitch spoke briefly over the radio to someone, asking for "clearance to taxi." The reply that came back sounded garbled to Serena, but Mitch apparently understood it because soon the small plane was rolling down the taxiway. When it stopped just short of the runway,

Mitch seemed to be going through some kind of checklist. Although several questions sprang to her mind, she resisted the urge to ask them, fearing that if she distracted him, he might overlook some vital step in the procedure.

Once again he spoke over the radio, his voice low and self-assured. "This is Cherokee 53 Foxtrot, ready for takeoff."

This time the reply was easier to understand. "Hold your position, 53 Foxtrot. We have an aircraft on final."

Another airplane, obviously the one "on final," landed in front of them, and Serena watched as it gradually slowed down. After another brief exchange with the tower, Mitch put the Cherokee in motion again, and in a short time they were moving down the runway, picking up speed.

Once they were airborne, Serena let her breath out slowly. This wasn't nearly as frightening as she'd expected it to be, she realized as she watched the landscape fall away below them. Actually, it was rather pleasant. She almost blurted this out, but caught herself in time to bite the words off. Mitch's demeanor did not invite conversation. In fact, he seemed almost oblivious to her presence.

With a little shrug, she turned toward the window. If he preferred to make the entire trip without talking, that was fine with her. She wouldn't dream of forcing her attention on him.

After a while the steady drone of the engine became monotonous, and her thoughts began to wander. . . .

* * *

It was hard to believe it had been just a little over a week since that thick, official-looking envelope had come in the mail.

"It's from a lawyer—Ralph Hubbard," her roommate and best friend, Kelly O'Hara, had commented as she'd brought in the mail. "In Cougar Bluff, Idaho—wherever that is."

"Um-hmm," Serena had murmured absentmindedly. "Just put it on the table with the rest of the mail."

Kelly hadn't bothered to hide her curiosity. "Aren't you even going to open it?"

"Later," Serena replied, her attention on the stack of papers she was grading.

"If you aren't the limit! You get a letter from a lawyer, and you don't even *glance* at it. For all you know, somebody could be suing you."

"Oh, Kelly, don't be silly." But Serena's exasperation was tempered with affection. She was more amused than offended by her friend's blatant curiosity. They were closer than many sisters and had shared secrets and confidences since junior high. At least life with Kelly was never dull. Trust her to make a big deal out of an everyday incident.

"Well, if you're not even curious, I am." Squinting, the irrepressible redhead held the envelope up against the light. "There's something in here about—"

"You're impossible," Serena scolded, with good-natured resignation. Shaking her head, she put aside her papers and pen and took the envelope from Kelly.

"I don't suppose you'll give me a moment's peace until the big mystery is solved." She carefully worked the envelope flap open and drew out the sheaf of papers inside, while Kelly hovered impatiently at her elbow. "I'm sure it's nothing important. You know, they put junk mail in official-looking envelopes these days." As she spoke she unfolded the papers and glanced at the one on top. "They do that so people will think. . . ."

Her words trailed off as her customary composure deserted her.

"Serena, what is it?" Kelly's teasing manner of a few seconds earlier gave way to concern as she noted her friend's stricken expression.

"It's my father. He—he's dead. He had a heart attack."

"Your father?" Kelly's tone indicated her surprise. "I thought the only contact you'd ever had with him was through the support checks he sent while you were growing up. How did this lawyer know where to find you?"

Serena shook her head. "I have no idea. Apparently *he's* kept track of *me* over the years, even after I was grown and the support checks stopped. I suppose if my name and address were found among his possessions, whoever is managing his affairs must have felt obligated to notify me. As far as I know, I'm his only surviving relative."

"What else does the letter say?"

Still dazed, Serena replied, "Why—I don't know. I only got as far as the part about his death. Why don't you take a look?'' She handed the papers over to Kelly. ''Is there anything there about when the funeral is to be held?''

Kelly scanned the letter, picking out phrases. '' ' . . . buried privately . . . in accordance with his wishes . . . ' '' she read. ''I guess that means the funeral has already taken place.'' A frown creased her forehead as she continued reading, attempting to translate the legal jargon into everyday language as she went along. ''Omigosh!'' Her eyes widened. ''According to this, your father left you his ranch!''

''His ranch?'' Serena echoed in bewilderment. ''Why would he leave it to *me*? We never even knew each other.''

''Whether or not you knew each other, he was still your father,'' Kelly reminded her. ''As you just pointed out, you're his only relative.''

''But what in the world am I going to do with a ranch in Idaho?''

''Just a minute. There's more.'' Kelly quickly read on down the page. ''He says there's someone who is interested in buying it. He feels it would be in your best interests to accept the offer, and his firm would be happy to act as your agent. He's enclosing a description of the inheritance, along with the proposed conditions of the sale. If the terms meet with your approval, he'll send you the papers to sign, authorizing him to act in your behalf. In any case, he'd like you to contact him at your earliest convenience.''

She riffled through the sheaf of papers until she

located the documents in question. She and Serena examined them together.

"I can see this inheritance isn't going to elevate me to the ranks of the 'idle rich,' " Serena commented as she and Kelly studied the neat columns of figures, which listed the ranch's debts and liabilities as well as assets. There seemed to be more of the former. Apparently the cattle business was a shaky venture, at best.

Serena had always taken her father's financial support for granted, but it occurred to her now that it may not have always been easy for him to fulfill his obligation to her. Yet she couldn't recall one instance, the entire time she was growing up, when the support check from her father hadn't arrived on schedule.

After their perusal of the ranch's financial state and the terms of the sale, Serena and Kelly turned their attention to the will, which was also enclosed. It was fairly straightforward. Charles Cole, being of sound mind, et cetera, left his entire estate, including the Double C Ranch—along with the house, outbuildings, livestock, and equipment—to his daughter, Serena.

"Wow!" Kelly was clearly impressed. "If there's someone who wants to buy the place, you'd better call this lawyer and tell him to go ahead with the sale before the buyer changes his mind. Here's the number on the letterhead."

Serena reached for the telephone but found herself hesitating. She wasn't sure why. The terms of the sale certainly sounded generous enough, even though she was inexperienced in such matters. . . .

A subtle change—some slight difference in the airplane's altitude or direction—brought Serena's attention back to the present. She glanced out the window and saw that they were slowly banking to the right. Mitch still hadn't made any attempt at conversation. In fact, he may as well have been alone in the cockpit, for all the attention he was paying to her.

She noticed that some of the rocky terrain below was giving way to large, flat areas, dotted with placidly grazing cattle. A silver ribbon of creek meandered here and there, disappearing between two rugged outcroppings of granite before it reappeared farther down, where the land smoothed out.

"Is that part of the Double C?" she asked, her curiosity overcoming her determination to show Mitch she could remain every bit as aloof as he.

"No, that's Diamond T land."

A map had been included in the material from the lawyer, and now she tried to picture it in her mind. She recalled that the Diamond T adjoined her property, but she couldn't remember in which direction it lay. She leaned forward so she could look past Mitch to see out the other window. "What's out that way?"

"That's Diamond T too."

All she wanted was a glimpse of the land that now belonged to her, but apparently getting any information out of this taciturn man was going to be like playing Twenty Questions. "Well, where is the Double C?" she persisted.

"It starts just on the other side of that stand of pines."

She located the dark, bristly clump of trees he'd indicated. They were easy to spot because off to one side of them an unusual rock formation rose high into the air like a silent sentinel.

"Will we be flying over the Double C?"

He shook his head. " 'Fraid not." His manner indicated that his patience was being sorely tried by so many questions.

"Oh." She wondered just how far they *were* going. Although she was disappointed that she wouldn't get to view her property from the air, she wouldn't dream of asking him to do her a favor and go out of his way. She settled for leaning forward as far as her seat belt would allow, straining for a brief glimpse of her land.

"You'll be able to see part of the Double C from here."

Serena stole a quick glance at Mitch. This was the first bit of information he'd offered voluntarily. Did the man actually have a bit of human kindness in him?

"See that low ridge off in the distance?" he went on. "Double C land extends to just beyond that point."

As Serena looked off in the direction he'd indicated, she was overcome with a sudden rush of emotion. In spite of never having been here before, she had a sensation of "coming home." Inexplicably, a lump came to her throat, and her eyes began to feel watery. She blinked several times to stem the unexpected tears that threatened to spill over.

Mitch glanced at her curiously but said nothing, and Serena kept her chin high and her eyes straight ahead.

Now it was her turn to maintain an attitude of detachment.

When she had her emotions sufficiently under control again, she took a closer look at the Double C. The packet of papers from the lawyer had included a legal description of her property, with the total area given in acres. Although she hadn't been able to translate the figures into anything she could relate to, she'd supposed the Double C was comparable in size to the surrounding ranches. Yet it was obviously dwarfed by its nearest neighbor, the Diamond T.

"Who owns the Diamond T?" she asked.

"I do." He spoke the words flatly, and they just sort of hung there in the air.

Serena caught herself before her jaw dropped open in surprise. She wondered if the reason for his aloof attitude was because his holdings were so much larger than hers. *So, big deal,* she thought. Who did he think he was, anyway—some kind of feudal lord? Didn't he realize this was the twentieth century?

She tried to frame some suitably scathing remark about those who looked down on others who weren't as wealthy. Her attention was diverted, however, as a slight shift in the Cherokee's direction of travel brought an elongated clearing into view. She could see a blue-and-white Blazer parked to one side, looking, from this distance, like a toy. It wasn't until Mitch had maneuvered the plane into position that Serena realized he meant to land down there.

Flanked on one side by trees and on the other by an irregular rock formation, the strip of land hardly seemed wide enough to accommodate a bicycle. As they began their descent, she instinctively closed her eyes but then opened them again, unwilling to display any sign of weakness to this infuriating man.

Her brief flash of apprehension soon dissipated as she glanced over at Mitch. His easy, self-assured movements as he guided the plane had a reassuring effect on her. In spite of his overbearing manner, the man did have a way of inspiring confidence.

## *Chapter Two*

Mitch landed the plane so smoothly that there was only the tiniest of bumps to indicate that the wheels had touched the ground. Then they were rolling down the landing strip, taxiing to a stop. By the time Serena had unbuckled her seat belt and climbed out of the Cherokee, Mitch had already had her bags transferred to the Blazer. She couldn't help thinking he certainly seemed to be in a hurry, as if he couldn't wait to deliver her to her destination so he could get on to more important matters. To be entirely fair, she could hardly blame him. He undoubtedly had better ways to spend his time than playing chauffeur for someone who—at least from his point of view—had no business here in the first place.

Once again the thought crossed her mind that it had been a mistake to make this trip. She didn't belong here. Why hadn't she simply accepted the offer on her ranch, signed the papers, and let the lawyer handle the entire matter? What had she hoped to accomplish by insisting on seeing the place for herself before irrevocably signing it away?

"Ready?" Mitch asked, his deep voice breaking into her thoughts. He was looking at her expectantly as he held the door of the Blazer open. Embarrassed at having caused him even a small delay, Serena hurried to take her seat in the sturdy four-wheel-drive vehicle. Almost before she was buckled in, Mitch had the engine started.

They traveled a short distance along a trail of packed earth. Then Mitch maneuvered the Blazer onto a narrow dirt road that curved and snaked its way around outcroppings of rock and up and down steep inclines. Serena stared in wonder at the constantly changing landscape. Jagged peaks gave way to brush-lined gullies and ravines that, in turn, became stark, barren prairies, dotted with an occasional herd of cattle off in the distance. In spite of the rugged beauty, the land seemed lonely and inhospitable.

*No wonder my mother was so unhappy here,* Serena thought.

It was almost dark when Mitch brought the Blazer into a sharp right turn that caused Serena to clutch the edges of her seat. She let her breath out slowly when she saw that he hadn't been seized with a sudden urge to go hurtling across this rugged backcountry to—goodness knew where. There actually was a road, although it was almost hidden by the thick brush that grew on either side of it. She hoped he hadn't noticed her sudden flash of panic, but his quick, amused glance told her he had.

"Well, there it is," Mitch said a short time later.

They had topped a small rise, and she could see a house and several outbuildings spread out in the valley below, looking like a set for a movie or a TV program. Serena had time to take in the entire scene as he slowed to negotiate a curve and eased the Blazer down the steep incline.

A corral near the barn held a couple of horses, and a battered green pickup truck was in the driveway. In the gathering darkness, Serena could just make out the figure of a man leaning across the front fender, his head under the open hood, obviously examining the vehicle's inner workings. A large golden dog in the yard glanced up at them with interest.

At their approach the man who was tinkering with the truck turned around and straightened, massaging the small of his back. He pulled a greasy rag from his back pocket and wiped his hands on it as Serena alighted from the Blazer. She knew, even before he said a word, that this could be none other than Farley. The grizzled, weather-beaten face and short, slightly bowlegged figure had to go with the gravelly voice she'd heard over the phone.

"You'd be Charlie's young'n." The old man stepped forward to greet her. "I'm pleased to make your acquaintance, Miz Cole," he said, with a sort of courtly charm that immediately endeared him to Serena.

*Charlie's young'n.* Although Serena hardly considered herself a "young'n," the phrase had a nice ring to it. "Please call me Serena," she replied, taking the gnarled hand he extended. "And you're Mr. Farley. I'm glad to meet you."

"Not 'Mister.'"

"I beg your pardon," she murmured, puzzled by this cryptic remark.

"Not Mister Farley, ma'am. Jes' Farley."

"Oh. I see." Actually, she didn't. She had no idea whether Farley was his first or his last name.

The dog had managed to work his way in between Serena and Farley, as if waiting to be introduced. "This's Max," Farley informed her. "He helps look after things around here." The plumed tail waved in majestic dignity as Serena patted his silky head.

By this time Mitch had her bags unloaded. As she turned to thank him, he was already getting back into the Blazer.

"Appreciate your giving Miz Cole a lift," Farley called after him.

"No problem." He waved an arm out the window as he turned the Blazer around and headed back up the driveway. "Glad to do it."

*I'll bet,* Serena thought, but she managed a polite "Thank you," just before he was out of earshot.

"Now then," Farley said, picking up her suitcases and heading for the house, "let's get you settled."

As he opened the back door and stepped aside to let her enter, Serena prepared herself for what she expected to be the typical bachelor's quarters. To her surprise, everything seemed reasonably neat and tidy, although a light layer of dust covered the tabletops and other surfaces.

"I brought in a few groceries," Farley said. "I—ah—wasn't sure what you'd need—not knowing how long you're planning to stay. . . ."

His voice trailed off, and Serena had that feeling once again that she was complicating things for everyone else by coming here. Until she went ahead with the sale of the ranch, Farley and the other employee—Homer—couldn't get on with their own lives. And Farley probably felt obligated to look after her.

Farley set the suitcases down inside the door. "Bedrooms are down the hall. If you need anything, jes' holler. I'll be right out back."

"I'll be fine," Serena assured him.

Once Farley had gone out, she wandered into the living room and surveyed her surroundings. The large room was paneled in some kind of wood, and a massive stone fireplace ran along one wall. Although the furnishings were somewhat shabby, they exuded a homey, down-to-earth air. She yawned deeply. She wasn't sure if it was the folksiness of the place that was affecting her or if her sudden weariness was due to her long trip, but all at once she could hardly hold her eyes open. After all, she reminded herself, her system was still on East Coast time, and it was three hours later there.

She was just starting down the hallway in search of the bedrooms when a chorus of insane screams cut through the silence. The high-pitched sounds made the hair on the back of her neck stand straight up and chilled her to the very marrow of her bones. Her heart thudding against her ribs, she raced through the kitchen to the back door and flung it open. She was about to run outside in search of—she wasn't sure what—when the sight of Farley brought her to a halt. He was staring disconsolately into the pickup truck's engine, scratching his chin. He looked up in surprise as the door flew open.

"Th-there's something out there," she stammered, making an effort to regain her composure. "I—I heard it."

"That's jes' a pack of coyotes." He pronounced it *KI-otes*. "They make a lot of noise, but they won't hurt you. You'll get used to the sound."

"Of course," she murmured. "I'm sure I will." She backed into the kitchen and closed the door. She was trembling, and her legs felt almost too weak to support her.

As her breathing and pulse rate returned to normal, she resumed her tour of the house. The first door she opened off the hallway revealed a bedroom with a lived-in look, as if its occupant had just stepped out and would return momentarily. That would be her father's room, of course. She closed the door softly and continued down the hall. There would be time enough to explore later. The next door opened into what was obviously the spare bedroom. By the time she'd found sheets and blankets and made up the bed, she all but fell into it.

In spite of her weariness, sleep eluded her, however. In her mind she kept going over the rest of that conversation with Kelly the day the letter had come. . . .

* * *

Serena had hesitated about calling Mr. Hubbard to tell him to go ahead with the sale.

"Something wrong?" Kelly had asked, looking at her curiously.

"It's just that—well, you know I never knew my father. You've heard the whole story, of course, of how my parents divorced before I was born and my dad went back to Idaho while Mom stayed here and had me—so you know this ranch is all I have left of him. It just seems so—sort of cut and dried to sign it away, just like that."

"But he must have known when he left it to you that you wouldn't be able to run the place," Kelly pointed out reasonably. "Surely he didn't expect you to keep it."

"That's just it," Serena countered. "Maybe he did. If he just wanted me to have the money from the sale of the ranch, why didn't he just stipulate in his will that the ranch was to be sold when he died, with the proceeds going to me?"

"I don't know. Maybe it just never occurred to him." Kelly sounded slightly exasperated, as if her friend weren't behaving quite rationally and it was her duty to keep Serena from doing anything foolish. "But if you have the chance to sell, you'd better snap it up. If you take too long and the buyer backs out, you'll be stuck with a cattle ranch."

"If it's a valid offer, I doubt if it'll be withdrawn just because I want a little while to think it over. Don't forget, until a few minutes ago I didn't even know I had a cattle ranch. I'm at least entitled to a few days to enjoy the feeling of being a landowner.''

''Just don't wait too long,'' Kelly warned. ''Don't forget, the operative word here is cattle—as in *cows*. If it were just a piece of land and some buildings, you could put everything on hold while you sort out your feelings, but those cows aren't going to go into suspended animation in the meantime.''

Kelly had a good point. Still, Serena couldn't quite bring herself to make the phone call that would sever her last connection with the father she'd never known. Preserving this link seemed especially important in view of the fact that she'd lost her mother two years earlier. The sense of loss when her mother was killed in an automobile accident had been softened slightly by the awareness, somewhere in the back of her mind, that at least she still had a father, even if she'd never met him. Now she was faced with the realization that she was quite alone in the world.

Secretly, she'd always cherished the hope that she might someday establish some sort of relationship with her father. She wasn't sure just when or how this would come about—there were no guidelines for this sort of thing. Now it was too late, and she felt a pang of sadness for what might have been, for the opportunity that was lost to her forever. If she made that phone call to the lawyer in Idaho, telling him to go ahead with the sale, she'd be eliminating this one last link with her heritage.

''Don't you see, Kelly?'' She tried to explain. ''He was giving me the only thing he had.''

"But it would have gone to you, anyway, even if he hadn't left a will," Kelly pointed out.

"That's just the point." Serena's tone was thoughtful, and there was a faraway look in her eyes. "By going through the formality of making me his heir, it's as if he were making me a gift of the only thing he owned of any value. Oh, I know I can't keep it—there's no way I could run a ranch. But it doesn't seem right to let it go without even having set eyes on it. Before I sell it, I'd like to at least see it. . . ."

Her voice trailed off as she caught her friend's expression. She hadn't really expected Kelly to understand when she herself didn't, but she had the vague feeling that if she could at least visit the ranch her father had loved, could walk where he'd walked and breathe the same air he'd breathed, she might somehow feel closer to him.

Eventually, of course, she had made her telephone call to Mr. Hubbard. "I'd like to take a trip out there and look over the ranch before I sign the final papers authorizing the sale," she'd explained to him in what she hoped was a businesslike manner, striving to sound as if she were experienced in the buying and selling of property.

"Certainly," he'd replied. "Let me know when you plan to arrive, and I'll arrange for someone to meet you and take you to the ranch. And—ah—Miss Cole, keep in mind that this is a working ranch. Your father's two employees, Farley and Homer, have agreed to stay on to keep things going until the final disposition is made, but. . . ."

Although he had left the rest of the sentence dangling, it wasn't difficult to fill in what he'd left unsaid—that the sooner she quit this foot-dragging, the sooner others could get on with the serious business of running a cattle ranch. She almost considered giving up the idea as foolish and impractical. But she found herself being carried along by something that went beyond logic or reason.

Getting time off to make the trip was no problem, since she hadn't yet secured a permanent position after acquiring her teaching degree. She had the promise of one in the fall, and in the meantime she was taking temporary assignments as a substitute teacher. With her current commitment due to end soon, there was no reason why she couldn't allow herself a few weeks off.

She cringed slightly when she realized how the plane fare would deplete her already tiny emergency fund. She eased her thrifty New England conscience, however, by reminding herself that she could replace the money once the sale of her property was completed.

Serena awoke to bright-yellow sunshine falling across her pillow. For just a second she felt a ripple of apprehension at the realization of where she was. It disappeared as soon as she bounded out of bed, however. From her window she could see a low, jagged ridge off in the distance, starkly silhouetted against the morning light. All at once she was eager to be up and about, to explore this interesting new place.

After a quick shower she dressed in a trim blue-plaid cotton shirt and her favorite denim jeans. She studied her reflection in the mirror as she tied her hair back with a square of cloth in the same shade of blue as her shirt. *Not too bad,* she decided. Except for the Nikes on her feet, she didn't look too much like an outsider. Last night she'd noticed a box filled with assorted boots just inside the back door. Maybe she could find a pair in her size.

At first she felt like an intruder as she prepared a quick breakfast—as if she were poking around in someone else's kitchen. But then she reminded herself that this was *her* house, at least for the time being. When she was finished eating, she rummaged around in the box of boots until she found some that fit her. She felt very western as she studied the tops of her feet in the scuffed boots. Satisfied that she didn't look terribly out of place, she stepped outside to explore her new surroundings.

She decided to begin her tour with the barn. As she approached the weathered structure with Max, the big golden dog, falling into step beside her, she was startled by a figure that materialized from the shadowy interior.

"Oh!" She gave a little cry of surprise.

"Sorry, ma'am," Farley apologized. "I didn't mean to scare you. Saw you coming, and I was stepping out to say howdy."

"I was just coming outside to look the place over. Uh—just one thing before I start poking around," she said. "Which building is the bunkhouse?" Last night when they'd driven in, she hadn't seen anything that looked like one, and she didn't want to stumble onto it by mistake.

"Well, there ain't one. Y'see, on a spread as small as this'n, we don't have enough hands to need a bunkhouse."

"But who does all the work, then?"

Farley gave a little shrug, looking almost embarrassed at her innocent question. "Me'n Homer do most of it—and Charlie, of course, before he died. I bunk in that little trailer out behind the barn"—he glanced in that direction—"and Homer don't live here at the ranch. He has a place of his own between here and town."

Serena recalled movies she'd seen of large groups of cowboys roping and branding cattle. "With only two ranch hands, what do you do at—uh—roundup time?"

"On the big spreads—like the Diamond T—they can afford to hire lots of help. Most of the ranches around here are small two- or three-man operations like this one, though, so we help each other, especially during roundup. We all get together to do one man's range and then move on to the next, and so on," he explained. "None of these small places could stay in business unless we all worked together."

Well, so much for her illusions about cattle ranching, Serena thought wryly.

" 'Course, Charlie sometimes hired temporary help for the bigger jobs that are too much for three people to handle alone," Farley went on. "During haying season, for instance, he'd always get in a neighbor kid or two to help out."

"Is that a sideline?" she asked. "The hay, I mean."

She thought the ranch's primary business was raising Hereford cattle.

"Oh, no, ma'am. On a ranch, raising hay ain't just a sideline. Y'see, that's what gets the cattle through the winter, when the grazing gets scarce."

"Oh." She felt terribly naive. She wished she'd done a little advance research about ranching, so she wouldn't have to have these basic facts explained to her.

"By the way, Mitch Tanner dropped by before you was up. Wanted to see you."

*Goodness, the man must leap out of bed at the crack of dawn,* Serena thought. She herself had been up fairly early. "Did he mention what he wanted?"

"Nope. Just said to tell you he'd come by this evening."

Serena couldn't imagine what reason Mitch would have for wanting to come over. Of course, it was entirely possible that he merely intended to pay her a neighborly visit, but somehow he didn't seem the type to waste time on social amenities.

"C'mon, I'll show you around the place," Farley said, cutting into her thoughts.

"Great! Let's get started," she replied. There was time enough later to puzzle out why Mitch Tanner wanted to see her.

Farley's sight-seeing tour included, among other things, the barn itself, where Serena was enchanted by the litter of kittens that staged mock battles in the hay; the tack shed, with its bewildering array of equipment; and the large corral behind the barn, where a bay mare with an intelligent expression came up to the fence and nuzzled them curiously.

"This's Lady," Farley said, pride apparent in his voice and manner. "The boss had her bred last year. She'll foal in another month or so. We been keeping her close by so we can keep an eye on her. Don't want nothing to go wrong. With her good blood lines, her foal should bring a good price."

She realized that Farley was looking at her expectantly, waiting for her opinion on what was obviously an outstanding example of horseflesh. She stepped back to survey the animal with what she hoped looked like a practiced eye.

"Quarter horse?" she asked tentatively.

"That's right. I see you know your horses."

Although Farley sounded somewhat surprised, Serena sensed that she had won his approval. She hoped her relief wasn't too obvious. She suppressed a brief twinge of guilt—the old man's pleased expression convinced her the slight subterfuge was justified. Besides, her remark about Lady's being a quarter horse hadn't been just a shot in the dark. When she and Kelly were teenagers and were going through their "horsey" period, they'd *devoured* books and magazines about horses, and she recalled seeing pictures of quarter horses and reading that they were compact and well-muscled.

"D'ya ride, may I ask?"

"Why, yes," she replied. "As a matter of fact, I do." At least she was on safe ground there. During her teenage years she and Kelly had spent several summers mucking out stalls at Shamrock Stables in Windham, in return for riding lessons. Although she didn't consider herself an expert by any means, she was reasonably confident of her ability to handle a horse.

"I was going to ask if there is a horse around here that can be spared. I'd like to ride out and look the place over."

Farley's weather-beaten face broke into a wide grin. "We should have something around here on four legs that's about right for a young lady. I know just the thing! Charlie had this pretty little mare that he took in a trade, and nobody around here rides her much,'cause she's a mite too small for a man. Used to belong to a lady rancher who had to let her go when she moved back to town. She's real gentle and neck-reins real easy, but has just the right amount of spirit. She's down in the lower pasture. I can go get her if you'd like."

"No, you don't have to do that right now. Maybe tomorrow. I thought I'd spend today just looking around close to the house." Although Serena appreciated the time Farley was taking to make her feel welcome, she knew he had his own chores to attend to. "Thanks for the tour. I'll let you get on with your work now."

She spent the rest of the day exploring the house. As she wandered through the rooms, touching and examining, she tried to imagine her father in these surroundings, relaxing in that easy chair in the evenings or having a cup of coffee at the wooden table in the kitchen. She didn't even have a clear image of what he looked like. Her only picture of him was a grainy black-and-white snapshot, surreptitiously salvaged from a pile of discards destined for the trash pickup when she was still a child. She hadn't been able to tell much about his actual physical appearance from that picture, but she'd somehow sensed that he was a quiet, gentle-spoken man.

Eventually her tour of the house took her to her father's bedroom, which was almost Spartan. It was easy to see he'd been a down-to-earth man, with simple tastes. The only thing out of place was a plaid flannel shirt hanging over the back of a straight-backed chair. It was likely the last thing he'd worn. She gathered it close to her and inhaled deeply. It had a masculine scent of soap and leather and horses. Suddenly she thought of all those wasted years that could never be recaptured, and she was almost overwhelmed with a sense of loss.

She hadn't realized she was crying until she glanced down at the garment in her hands and saw drops of moisture on it. She made no attempt to hold back the tears. Allowing them to flow freely was a relief. When she was finally all cried out, she felt as if she'd been through a sort of cleansing. After a while she dried her eyes and continued with her exploration.

Tucked away on the top shelf of a closet was an old photograph album. She opened it eagerly and exclaimed with delight when she found that the pictures dated back to the early days of her parents' marriage. Along with shots of scenes around the ranch, there were some of her mother standing in the doorway of the barn, sitting on the tractor and even astride a horse.

And there were several of her parents with their arms around each other, looking so much in love that Serena's vision misted over again and a lump came to her throat.

Except for the pictures of her father and mother together, it seemed that her father was inclined to be somewhat camera-shy. She did find a few shots of him leaning against a fence or standing in front of the house, smiling self-consciously. She held these under the light and studied them closely, but the faded old photographs revealed little of the person behind that touchingly boyish face.

Serena felt a sense of loss when she discovered that the pictures tapered off about one third of the way through the album and that the rest of the pages were blank.

On the same shelf with the album she found a thick notebook. It had the same kind of hardcover binding as a ledger, and she expected it to contain accounts of ranch expenditures. When she discovered it was a journal, written by her father in longhand, her heart began to thud as if she had just come across hidden riches.

A quick glance revealed that the entries were, for the most part, random thoughts—one passage described a sunset that had particularly moved him—or accounts of everyday happenings, such as, . . . *spotted an elk down by the water hole last night* . . . or, . . . *looks like the first snowfall is on the way*. . . .

She resisted the urge to drop everything and read

the notebook all the way through. She wanted to wait until she had time to savor each word.

By the time a few early-evening shadows were starting to creep into the corners of the old house, she'd begun to feel a closeness with her father, a sense of the kind of man he'd been. As she examined his home and belongings, his presence seemed almost to surround her. She allowed herself to imagine what her life might have been like if she and her father had had the opportunity to get to know each other.

Although this was an area she had always shied away from delving into too deeply, she now gave her imagination free rein. She could picture the two of them riding across the prairie together as she assisted him with his ranch chores, or having long, serious talks in front of the fireplace in the evenings.

So engrossed was she in her fantasy that she was surprised when she glanced out the window and saw Mitch's Blazer pull into the driveway. She'd completely forgotten that he'd told Farley he would drop by this evening.

She knew he was likely here on some kind of ranch business. Still, she couldn't resist watching him as he walked across the yard with long, purposeful strides. He seemed even taller than she remembered, more imposing.

And more attractive. The thought sprang to her mind, unbidden.

For just a second she found herself wishing she'd taken time to run a comb through her hair and dab on a bit of lipstick. Then she caught herself with a rueful, almost embarrassed laugh. The man wasn't here to court her, for goodness' sake. He was probably going to tell her something like, "Your fence is down, and your cattle are straying onto my grazing land." The realization brought on an unexpected stab of disappointment.

## *Chapter Three*

"Hi," Serena greeted Mitch as she opened the door to his knock. "Please come in."

" 'Evening." He removed his broad-brimmed hat as he stepped inside.

*Now what?* Serena wondered. She had no idea why he was here. Any passing thought she'd had that his visit might have been prompted by neighborly friendliness was quickly eliminated by his businesslike demeanor. Well, whatever his reason for coming, they could still behave in a civilized manner, she decided.

"Would you like some coffee?" she asked.

"No, thank you, Miss Cole."

"Why not call me Serena?" she suggested, striving for a light, informal tone. "After all, we *are* neighbors, at least for a little while. We may as well be on a first-name basis."

"Serena," he amended with a slight shrug, as if the matter of names were of little importance.

She suppressed the surge of resentment that rushed

through her. "Would you like to sit down?" she asked, still determined to observe the amenities.

"No, I'll stand. This isn't a social call, Miss Co— Serena. It's business."

She refrained from pointing out that where she came from, even business matters were conducted with a certain degree of civility and courtesy. She'd tried, hadn't she? What was wrong with him? "Well, then, how may I help you?" she asked, retreating behind an attitude of impersonal haughtiness.

"I'll get right to the point. I'd like to know why you turned down my offer to buy the Double C."

*His* offer? So he was the "interested party" Mr. Hubbard had referred to. She felt he'd been unnecessarily secretive by not mentioning this on the ride out to the ranch yesterday. Caught off guard, she was too surprised to know just what to say. She needed a little time to process this new bit of information.

"I suppose you're holding out for more money," he commented, apparently misunderstanding her silence. "If you are, you'll have trouble selling the place. The offer I made was a fair price."

Serena felt her temper rising. She resented his implication that she thought of her legacy merely in light of how much profit she could make from its sale. Under different circumstances she might have attempted to explain why it was important to her to at least see the ranch that had meant so much to her father, before signing it away. But his high-handed attitude triggered a streak of perverseness in her. She would reveal nothing of her inner feelings to him. Anyway, she was getting a little tired of being made to feel as if she were under some obligation to sell the ranch as soon as possible, just so nobody else would be inconvenienced. It *did* belong to her, after all.

She couldn't resist a sudden urge to take him down a peg or two. "I came here to look over my property," she said, lifting her chin slightly, "and I won't be intimidated into making a hasty decision."

For just an instant his mask of restraint slipped, and the lines of his face tightened in a disapproving frown. To his credit, however, he quickly regained control of his emotions. "I see," he replied, with a little nod that she supposed was meant to indicate that their business discussion was finished. He strode to the door, then paused with his hand on the knob to look back at her.

"Don't wait too long," he advised in clipped tones. "This isn't a game, you know. There are decisions that need to be made concerning management of the ranch, and those cattle won't wait around while you play at being a rancher." Then he turned and went out.

Serena was so angry, she was sorely tempted to throw something. She even went so far as to grab a small, heavy paperweight off the desk. But no matter how satisfying it would have been to heave it at his retreating form, she knew it wasn't really in her nature to take her anger out in a physical manner. Instead, she usually assumed an air of chilly reserve. Ashamed at having almost lost control of her emotions that way, she stared at the object she had unthinkingly picked up, actually seeing it for the first time.

Viewed from one side it appeared to be an ordinary, garden-variety rock—rough and irregular. But when she turned it over, she saw that it had been cut in half, and the inside had a delicate, greenish tint. The cut surface was highly polished and had an attractive, lacy pattern.

*Much too interesting to be wasted by being thrown at someone as high-handed and disagreeable as Mitch Tanner,* she thought as she replaced it on the desk.

She was glad she'd planned to be here no longer than a few weeks. During that time she would do her best to avoid Mitch. That shouldn't be too difficult, with all this open space around. And just before she left, she would contact Mr. Hubbard and advise him to go ahead with the sale. But Mitch Tanner needn't know of her intentions. *Let him stew a while,* she decided. It would do him good.

Serena was enchanted the next morning when Farley introduced her to Penny, who was indeed a "pretty little mare" with her gleaming chestnut coat and flaxen mane. Instant rapport was established when the dainty creature rubbed her velvety muzzle against Serena's shoulder, as if inviting friendship.

"Now, let's see if we can find some tack that'll fit." Farley disappeared into the tack shed and reappeared with a saddle, blanket, and bridle. "These should be about right. They're the smallest I could find." He balanced the saddle over the corral rail and positioned the blanket on Penny's back. Then he stepped back, and Serena realized, with dismay, that he was waiting for her to finish the job.

Although all the students at Shamrock Stables had been expected to saddle and bridle their own mounts, the enormous western saddle looked frighteningly unfamiliar to Serena, who was accustomed to the small English type. Her first impulse was to admit her confusion, but she caught herself. It somehow became very important for her to figure out, on her own, how to saddle Penny. As she studied the contraption of leather and wood and realized that it wasn't much different from an English saddle, some of her apprehension faded. She could, of course, ask Farley for help, but she was determined to manage on her own. In a way that she couldn't really explain, she felt that her honor was at stake.

Working slowly and deliberately, she managed to get the saddle and bridle on Penny. When she was finished, Farley checked her cinch, then nodded approvingly. She felt her confidence returning as she fitted the toe of her boot into the stirrup and swung her leg over Penny's back. She found that the western saddle was actually easier to mount, since there was a horn for her to grasp.

She started to gather up the reins in both hands, as she had been taught to do. Then, recalling pictures she'd seen, she instinctively adjusted her grip to hold the strips of leather in her left hand, while her free hand held the ends and kept them from dangling.

Serena found that Penny did, as Farley had said,

neck-rein ''real easy.'' Perfectly schooled, the little animal obeyed her rider's slightest command as Serena guided her with a combination of signals, including her hand on the reins, knee pressure, and balance. As she became accustomed to Penny's movements, she nudged her into a trot, moving up and down in the saddle in rhythm with the horse's movements.

Suddenly she became aware that Farley was standing stock-still, watching her. The expression on his face was one of stunned surprise.

''If you don't mind my askin', ma'am, what might ya be doin'?''

As she reined Penny to a halt, she recalled, somewhat tardily, that western riders didn't ''post.'' She had done it automatically, because that was the way she'd been taught to ride at a trot.

''I was—ah—posting,'' she explained lamely. ''It keeps the rider from being bounced around—''

''Posting,'' he echoed. ''No offense, ma'am, but around here that's just not the way we ride.''

She could feel her cheeks flaming, and she silently berated herself for making such a foolish mistake. ''I'll try to remember that.''

Serena spent the next hour or so on Penny, practicing different gaits until she was fairly certain she wouldn't forget herself and automatically start to post again. Farley watched her for a while and eventually seemed satisfied that she could be trusted to ride out by herself without losing her way or getting hurt.

''Just follow the trail out past that stand of pines yonder,'' he directed. ''You might take Max along for company. It's easy to lose your way around here, so if you do get lost, just give Penny her head. She'll bring you right back home. Watch your step—it's rained a lot lately, so the ground is slippery. Oh, and watch out for rattlesnakes."

*Rattlesnakes*! A shudder went through her. Besides having been frightened out of her wits by coyotes that first night, she also had to watch out for rattlesnakes!

Heedful of Farley's warning about getting lost, she paid careful attention to where she was going as she followed a natural trail that meandered through a stand of trees and skirted a shallow ravine. Occasionally, as the path twisted and curved around, she glimpsed dark clumps that she knew were cattle on distant hillsides.

Penny was careful about where she stepped, for which Serena was grateful. The spring thaw, along with the recent rains, had left the ground wet and muddy, with numerous puddles and slippery areas that could be dangerous. In spite of the mud, however, she was overwhelmed with her surroundings.

Once as she glanced up she saw a bird soaring above a rough granite cliff, silhouetted against the blue vault of sky. At first she thought it was a crow—its body appeared to be about that size—but a crow's wings wouldn't be those curving crescents that pointed downward at the tips. And a crow certainly wouldn't have such a wide wingspan. Why, this bird's wings must be at least three feet across! It must be some sort of hawk or falcon. Serena made a mental note to ask Farley.

As the bird wheeled about in a wide, curving arc,

the sun caught it and burnished its breast with gold. Suddenly, as if sighting something on the other side of the crag, it rose high into the air, then dived with almost unbelievable speed. Serena watched until it was out of sight before she rode on.

Eventually she found herself on the edge of a wide expanse of open land. To one side, a swollen stream rushed over a bed of boulders and gravel, and off in the distance peaks and ridges half filled the sky. It seemed to Serena's city-bred gaze as if a whole kingdom lay spread before her.

Introspective by nature, she found the solitude and sense of aloneness to be to her liking. She could readily understand, however, how her outgoing, fun-loving mother must have felt about this place. She recalled when she'd become old enough to wonder about the father she'd never known. She'd been nine or ten at the time—that was when her grandmother was still alive—and she'd instinctively taken her questions to Gram rather than to her mother.

"I always liked Charles. He's a good man," Gram had told her.

"Well, then, why didn't Mom stay married to him?"

"Your mother and father were just two different types of people. She tried living on his ranch, but she was utterly miserable. She'd grown up here in the East, you know, and she just couldn't adjust to life on a ranch in Idaho. And after she persuaded him to move back here, *he* was unhappy." Gram sighed, and a shadow crossed her face. "They were so much in love when they were first married, but they just couldn't reconcile their differences. When they reached the point where they were arguing constantly, they decided to separate.

"Charles went back to his beloved ranch, where he's been ever since. By that time you were on the way, of course, and there was no question about who should have custody, since your father was in no position to raise a child. I'm not saying I agree with their reasoning, mind you, but what's done is done."

"But hasn't my father ever even wanted to see me?" she persisted. Some of her friends whose parents were divorced were always going off to faraway places to visit one or the other absentee parent.

Gram's expression softened. "I'm sure he'd like to, honey, but in many ways it just wouldn't be practical. Your father has been living a bachelor life for years—he wouldn't know how to look after a little girl. And your mother probably wouldn't allow you to go there, anyway. She's convinced Idaho isn't part of the civilized world." The twinkle in Gram's eyes made it clear that she didn't entirely share her daughter's sentiments. "And as for Charles coming *here,* well, he might feel that you've already made a life without him, and he'd just be intruding. He was always kind of a shy, quiet man anyway. . . ."

By now the sun was directly overhead, and Serena realized she was more than ready for lunch. She was about to turn Penny around and head back, but something in the distance caught her eye. It was that odd column of rock she'd noticed from the airplane, just next to the stand of trees that separated her property from the Diamond T. Today she was seeing it from a different perspective, of course, but that unusual spire shape was unmistakable. She decided that before starting back, she would ride over as far as the boundary line. She nudged Penny into a trot, following the path of the stream that meandered toward the trees.

In a short time they reached the wooded area. As the little mare daintily picked her way along the carpet of pine needles, Serena was suddenly aware of a commotion of some sort just on the other side of a clump of thick brush. She reined Penny to a stop and listened carefully. There was a lot of rustling of branches and stomping, as if a large animal—or maybe several—might be milling around.

She tried to recall what kind of wildlife was native to Idaho. Bears? But a bear wouldn't stomp around that way. Anyway, she wasn't even sure if the bears had come out of hibernation yet. Elk? She seemed to remember that there *were* elk in this area. Did elk attack people? she wondered. While she was deciding whether to try to get out of the area as quietly as she could or to simply urge Penny into a gallop and put as much distance as possible between herself and *whatever* was making all that racket, the milling around seemed to subside and a new sound reached her ears.

It sounded like—but it couldn't possibly be—a man speaking in low, gentle tones. There was a soothing note to the voice, as if its owner were attempting to calm someone. Now more curious than frightened, Serena guided Penny ahead slowly, until they were brought up short by a barbed-wire fence, almost invisible in the thick bushes. Although this was as far as she could go in this direction, she was close enough to the clump of brush to peer through the branches and see what was taking place on the other side.

The scene that greeted her was like an illustration from a book about the Old West. The stream she'd been following came out on the other side of the trees and ran down a small slope. The low, wide area where it snaked around into an ess-curve had been turned into a muddy bog by the runoff, and a small calf was half submerged in the semisolid mess. Its forelegs were free, and from the way the mud around it was churned up, the animal had been frantically trying to get out. Now, apparently, it had all but given up. Its eyes had a glazed, empty look, and its head hung limply.

A horse stood just clear of the deeper mud, with a rope attached to its saddle horn. The other end of the rope was looped around the calf's chest. The horse's front legs were braced and, although he appeared to be standing completely still, every so often he moved almost imperceptibly, just enough to keep the rope taut.

Serena realized that she was watching a legendary cow pony, which had been perfectly trained and knew exactly what was expected of him. But what held her attention was the figure between the horse and calf. Mitch Tanner was gently tugging on the rope, with one booted foot planted solidly in the mud and the other leg slightly bent behind him for balance. He was covered with mud up to his knees, as if he had waded into the mudhole to tie the rope around the animal.

Every time he began to make a little progress toward pulling the calf out, it would rouse itself to set up a frantic scrambling, sometimes pushing itself deeper into the mire. Mitch kept up a steady monologue, crooning softly. Serena couldn't make out the words, but it was obvious from his tone that he was attempting to calm the poor, frightened creature. As she watched, she could see the animal starting to respond. Gradually its struggles ceased, and it allowed itself to be pulled free.

Once it was on relatively dry ground, Mitch untied the bandanna from around his neck and used it to carefully wipe the mud away from the calf's face, being especially gentle around the eyes and nose. While he did this, he was talking to the shivering animal in low, reassuring tones.

A warm feeling that Serena couldn't quite identify washed over her as she watched Mitch's ministrations. Why, he was as tender and compassionate with the calf as if it were a baby or a small child!

He made a quick but thorough examination of the animal, running his hands over its back and legs. Once he was satisfied that the creature was unhurt, he removed the rope, recoiled it, and attached it to the saddle by a length of leather that hung down.

Returning to the calf, he picked it up in his arms and gently placed it over the horse, with its front legs dangling down one side and its hind legs down the other. "Now, then, little feller," he said, swinging himself into the saddle, "let's go find your ma."

Serena stayed out of sight until he had ridden away;

then she turned Penny around and headed back toward the ranch. She was thoughtful as she rode. This Mitch Tanner she'd just seen, the one who could be so gentle and tender with a frightened baby animal, was inconsistent with her conception of him as cold and unfeeling.

# *Chapter Four*

Serena tried to crowd as much as possible into the short time she had allotted herself at the ranch. When the weather was nice, she saddled Penny and took long rides about the Double C, reveling in the vast distances and the breathtaking peaks and ridges that bordered the wide stretches of openness.

On rainy days she explored the house, getting a feel for the kind of man her father had been by examining his possessions. His books, for instance—a surprisingly varied assortment—gave her a picture of a quiet, thoughtful man whose feelings ran deep but who didn't easily express himself to outsiders.

In the evenings, when the darkness and the quiet closed in around her like a soft, warm blanket, she read from her father's journal. She skipped most of the passages that mentioned her parents' brief marriage. She would come back to them some other time, but right now she didn't want negative factors to mar her time here.

An entry dated several months after her parents'

separation read, *They tell me I'm the father of a baby girl. Serena, they call her. Pretty name. I wish things could have been different. . . .*

Serena sensed the sadness in that simple phrase.

After that she found her name mentioned frequently. *New kittens in the barn,* her father wrote. *Too bad Serena isn't here to enjoy them . . . kittens and little girls go together.* And another time, *Snowed pretty hard last night. If Serena were here, we'd build a snowman.* She was touched to discover she'd been in his thoughts so much. For some reason, she'd always assumed that, other than signing the support checks, he'd never really thought much about her.

By the time she came to, *My daughter turned thirteen today—she's not a little girl anymore,* she found herself wiping away tears.

The passage went on:

> *I wish we could have gotten to know each other, but every time I suggested having her come out for a visit, her mother had all kinds of reasons why it wouldn't be a good idea. ''Maybe later,'' she always said. I guess I should have insisted, but it's too late now. Serena is a young lady, and a city girl to boot. Probably the last thing she'd want to do is spend time on a broken-down old cattle ranch.*

He had cared about her, and wanted to get to know her! But her joy at this discovery was marred by a twinge of resentment. Even though she knew her mother hadn't kept them apart out of pettiness or spite, but had only done what she felt was best, Serena wished she'd at least been told that her father had wanted to see her. The knowledge would have meant so much to her.

The entry went on:

> *I'm sorry I never had the chance to show her this country and teach her to appreciate the silence and the vast openness; to help her learn to look inside herself and discover the inner peace that comes from being all alone out on the prairie when it seems you're the only person in the world. I wanted her to know how to be satisfied with the simple things in life.*

Now Serena made no attempt to wipe away the tears that were flowing unashamedly down her cheeks. A deep sadness came over her at learning that her father had had so much he wanted to share with her and had never been given the opportunity.

She had pictured her father as a shy, unassuming man, but she was seeing another side of him, a side she'd never known existed. It occurred to her that maybe the reason he'd made a point of leaving her the ranch in his will, even though he knew it would go to her, anyway, was because he'd hoped she'd come here and learn the things he'd never been given the chance to convey to her. And it had worked! She felt as if he were right here in the room, talking to her.

After that brief, self-revelatory passage, the entries reverted back to somewhat impersonal accounts of commonplace events, as if he had exposed more of his inner feelings than he'd meant to. Serena couldn't help thinking how like herself he must have been in that respect. She'd always been hesitant about revealing her private thoughts also.

One morning as Serena was approaching the barn, she overheard Farley grumbling to Homer about a fence-line that needed to be repaired. "One of us is gonna have to get out and do somethin' about that west fence," he was saying.

"Dunno when it's gonna get done," Homer replied. "Too many other jobs waitin' to be tended to."

"We can't move the herd until the fence is fixed," Farley pointed out. "If we did, we'd have cattle straying all over the county."

Serena listened to this conversation with dismay. It hadn't occurred to her how difficult it must be for the two ranch hands, trying to get around to all the chores that needed to be done. Of course they would be shorthanded, now that her father was gone. And here she was, contributing nothing. "Is there anything I can do to help?" she asked, stepping into the barn.

Farley looked at her in surpise, then shook his head. "Appreciate the offer, but mending fence is man's work."

"What does it involve?"

"If a section's actually broke, you gotta splice in a new piece of wire," he explained.

"Takes practice and know-how to be able to make a repair that'll stay together," Homer put in.

"I rode out that way the other day," Farley said.

"Didn't see any breaks in the wire—just places where it had come loose from the post."

"Then it's mostly a matter of nailing the loose wires back to the fence posts? That doesn't sound too difficult."

The two men exchanged glances. Farley spoke up first. "Aw, that ain't no job for a nice young lady."

"Why not?" she persisted. "I can probably handle a hammer as well as the next person. Surely it doesn't take a special skill to pound nails."

Although both men were skeptical, she eventually managed to convince them she wasn't a delicate hothouse flower, that a little honest physical labor wouldn't harm her in the least. They finally relented, and a little while later she was headed out toward the west fence, with the truck bed filled with tools, nails, wire cutters, and extra wire and her head full of more instructions and advice than she'd ever be able to remember.

She worked slowly and methodically. It was important to her to prove she could do the job properly. She was so engrossed in her task that she didn't notice the passage of time. It wasn't until her stomach began to protest that she realized she had worked straight through lunch.

That evening she had blisters on her hands, and her arms and shoulders were sore from using unaccustomed muscles, but she had a satisfying sense of having pulled her own weight.

A day or so later Farley checked her work, before the herd was to be moved. "Looks like you did a good job,'' he commented that evening. ''Didn't see any spots you missed, and all the repairs seem good and tight.''

After that Serena made it a point to help around the ranch as much as she could. She was beginning to see that there was a lot more to raising cattle than just putting them out on the range and letting them graze. There were many chores she had to leave to the two men, of course—she was aware that because of her inexperience she could sometimes do more harm than good. However, there were still a lot of odd jobs she *could* handle, freeing Homer and Farley for more important work.

One of the duties she took on as her own responsibility was tending weak or sickly calves that might not survive without special attention. Once Farley showed her what needed to be done—it was mostly a matter of keeping them warm and fed—she found that she had a special touch with the frail creatures. Several times she sat up all night in the shed, using infinite patience to coax the milk mixture down a calf that was too weak to nurse.

She realized that her two employees were in a difficult position, with the ranch ''between owners'' and nobody really in charge. For this reason she tried to make things as easy as possible for them by being as helpful as she could. Although neither man did anything to indicate he wished she would stop her foot-dragging and get on with the sale, she couldn't help feeling that everyone would be relieved once it took place.

Until the Double C was sold, it was in a state of limbo. Both Farley and Homer were experienced in all phases of ranching, but neither of them had the authority to make business decisions regarding the ranch's operation. And even though Serena had that authority, she knew nothing of ranching.

The two men had stayed on, of course, out of loyalty to her father, but how long could she expect them to continue in this state of uncertainty? They had their own lives to get on with. She had no idea whether Mitch planned on keeping them on when he became owner of the Double C or if they would have to look for new jobs, which wouldn't be easy at their ages.

Ralph Hubbard had called shortly after Serena's arrival and asked her to drop into his office sometime when she was in town. "There are several matters concerning your inheritance that need to be taken care of," he explained. "For instance, your father's bank account has to be closed out and a new one opened in your name, so checks can be written to pay the hands' salaries and other bills."

She wished she had demonstrated the business sense to have thought about these things herself. She should have asked what needed to be done to keep the ranch running smoothly until she was ready to sell it.

"I'll come in as soon as I can," she promised.

"I need to go into Cougar Bluff and see Mr. Hubbard," she mentioned to Farley a few days later. "I think I'll do that this morning if you're not planning to use the pickup truck. Is it very far?"

"About fifteen miles or so. Once you get up on the main road, just take a left, and it's a straight shot into town." He scratched his chin thoughtfully. "I'm not sure the truck'll make it that far and back, though. I put in that new distributor cap, but it still ain't running right."

But beneath Serena's mild exterior was a tough core of determination. "I think I'll chance it," she said decisively.

Fulfilling Ralph Hubbard's request wasn't her only reason for wanting to go into Cougar Bluff. She was curious to see the community that had been a part of her father's life. It had been his hometown and, as such, had helped form his personality. In spite of Farley's warning, she decided to take a chance that the truck would get her there and back. With her time here growing short, there wouldn't be many opportunities to go into the little town.

Farley's expression indicated his disapproval, but he merely shrugged, as if to say, *Suit yourself.* As he turned away, however, Serena heard him mutter something about, "Just like her pa—determined to do things her way." Although Serena realized Farley had meant his remark as a criticism, she was secretly pleased to be compared to her father.

A short time later Serena was behind the wheel of the beat-up old pickup, on her way into town. It was exhilarating, being out this early, when everything was still fresh and untouched. She had the windows down, and the clean breeze caressed her arms and teased her hair gently.

The shops and businesses were just opening when she arrived in Cougar Bluff. She found a parking spot, then strolled casually along the one main street on her way to Ralph Hubbard's office, stopping now and then to glance into store windows.

As she passed one little shop set back from the sidewalk, something drew her attention. The window display included an assortment of stones in their natural state, as well as cut, polished gems, some mounted as jewelry. But it was one piece in particular that had caught her eye. The stone, dangling from a delicate gold chain, was of such a deep, brilliant blue that it seemed to glow from within.

The reason she was so drawn to that one item was because she had a necklace with an almost identical stone. Her mother had handed it down to her when she'd reached her teens and was supposedly mature enough to be trusted with a "grown-up" piece of jewelry. All she knew of it was that her father had given it to her mother during their courtship and that her mother had never worn it after the divorce. She had, however, saved it to pass on to Serena.

"I have no idea if it's valuable," her mother had said. "Anyway, it's kind of pretty, so I thought you might like to have it."

Serena had been enchanted with the pretty blue stone, which, when the light touched it, glowed with a liquid intensity. There seemed to be something almost mystical about the way it revealed a faint star pattern when held at a certain angle. She recalled tilting it to catch a shaft of sunlight and watching the star as it seemed to move about inside the rounded surface of the stone.

Someone had once told her it was a star sapphire and fairly valuable. She'd never been sure, however. Most likely, it was merely a pretty piece of costume jewelry. Not that it mattered, anyway. It was valuable to *her,* simply because it had come from her father.

As she stood looking at the display, a gentle current of air set the gem moving slightly. It swung almost imperceptibly on its slender chain, catching the early-morning light slanting in through the window, until a star, deep inside, was clearly visible. Serena caught her breath. It *was* the same kind of stone.

The plump, middle-aged man in the shop raised his hand in a friendly gesture as he noticed Serena examining his display. As she returned the wave, his pleasant, round face broke into a smile of welcome. She took a few steps backward and looked up at the sign over the shop. *The Rockhound,* it read. On impulse she went inside.

The shopkeeper greeted her warmly. "Clarence Hicks is the name." He reached across the counter to shake her hand. "You must be Charlie Cole's daughter. Welcome to Cougar Bluff."

"Thank you. But how did you know—"

"Simple process of deduction. I know just about everybody who lives around Cougar Bluff, but I've never seen you before. And I heard Charlie's daughter was coming out here to look over the Double C. News travels fast around here,'' he added, noting her expression of surprise. ''Besides, you favor your father.''

Serena responded to that bit of information with a pleased smile.

''Saw you admiring my star sapphire,'' Clarence commented. ''You have good taste. That's a fine stone. Not too many of 'em left around here. By the way, did you know a sapphire's supposed to ward off evil forces and protect its wearer?''

''Why, no, I've never heard that.''

''That one in the window is one of the finest examples you're likely to see. It was found right here in Idaho, like all the other stones in my shop. 'Course, they're not all gem quality like that one. Most of the others I have are fairly common and not worth a lot, but some of 'em make up into pretty pieces of jewelry.''

''The reason I was looking at the star sapphire is because I have one like it,'' Serena explained.

''That right?'' Genuine interest was evident in his expression. ''Why not bring it in sometime and let me take a look at it? Could be you have something valuable. At one time there were a lot of sapphires to be found in this area—usually around gold-bearing gravels. That stone in the window was picked up near the remains of an old abandoned gold-mine operation like the one out on the Double C.''

Serena's eyes widened with interest. ''You mean there's actually a gold mine on my property?''

''Used to be, long time back. It was a placer mine—''

"Placer mine?" Serena wasn't familiar with the term.

"That means the gold was in a stream or creek. All a miner needed was a pick, a shovel, and a pan. Over the years all of 'em around here have been pretty well cleaned out, of course."

But even a used-up gold mine was interesting, Serena thought. "Do you know where the one on the Double C was located?"

"It was on what's now the boundary between your place and the Diamond T, but I doubt if there'd be anything left these days to even show where it was. Even the stream is dried up now. It was diverted for irrigation a long time ago, after the mine played out and the land was developed for ranching. I forgot to mention, I'm also sort of the unofficial local historian," he added.

"Do you think my sapphire—if that's what it is—might have come from there?"

"It's possible. That area was pretty rich with stones at one time. Not too likely you'd find anything of value out there these days, though. The gem hunters picked that spot clean years ago. In fact, it's getting harder and harder to find any really good stones. Oh, there might be a few to be found on private land, if a person knows what to look for, but most folks don't want a bunch of strangers running around on their property. A lot of 'em won't even allow the rockhounds on their land to look for the commoner stones, like garnet and quartz, for their collections. Can't say I blame 'em."

"But with all those thousands of acres out there,

why would the property owners object to people coming on their land to look for stones? I mean, if they're not worth anything, except to rock collectors. . . ."

Clarence rubbed his chin. "Well, even though the organized rockhound clubs are very careful not to disturb the environment, a few of the independent gem hunters have given all rockhounds a bad name. Some of them are just out to make a quick buck, and they get a little careless if they think they might find something valuable. They've been known to leave gates open or disturb livestock or leave garbage behind. It spoils things for the serious collectors."

"Are there a lot of rockhound clubs around here?" she asked.

"Oh, my, yes," Clarence replied, more than willing to enlighten her on a subject obviously dear to his heart. Apparently here in mineral-rich Idaho, collecting rocks and gems was a favorite hobby, not because of their value, but because it was an engrossing pastime. With such an interested audience, Clarence was a wealth of information. His small, crowded shop was lined with shelves displaying everything from "thunder eggs" to petrified wood, all neatly labeled.

"I have something like this too," Serena remarked, examining a rough, irregularly shaped rock with a cut, polished surface. It was similar to the paperweight she had almost thrown at Mitch.

"That's a piece of moss agate," Clarence explained. "It's not too valuable as a gem, but it's just a pretty thing to have around."

Before leaving the shop with a promise to drop in

again the next time she was in town, Serena bought a book on the rocks and gems of Idaho. The slim volume described the various minerals native to the state and even included maps of where they were likely to be found.

It was a relief to know that all the inhabitants of the area weren't as inhospitable as Mitch Tanner, she thought as she bade Clarence good-bye and went to look for Ralph Hubbard's office.

## *Chapter Five*

Ralph Hubbard welcomed Serena warmly. He was a tall, thin, older man with a reassuring commonsense air. Although he was dressed in a conventional business suit, Serena noticed the worn but well-polished boots showing below the bottoms of his trousers. *Boots seem to be almost obligatory footwear around here,* she thought.

"Thanks for coming by," he said when she'd completed her business with him. "Do you have any idea when you'll be ready to complete the sale of the ranch?" He gathered up the papers she'd just signed. "I don't mean to sound as if I'm rushing you. . . ."

"I'll be going home in about a week, so I'll take care of it just before I leave. I appreciate your patience. I know you'd like to get the whole matter settled, and I really *am* sorry to keep everyone waiting this way. But—well, once the ranch is sold, I'll never see it again. This is the only opportunity I'll ever have. . . ."

"I understand," he said. "It's just that I need to know what to tell the prospective buyer."

"Of course," Serena murmured. Recalling Mitch's

brief visit the day after her arrival, there were a few things *she* wouldn't mind telling him also.

"I notified him that you weren't quite ready to sell yet," Mr. Hubbard went on, "but somewhere along the way there seems to have been a breakdown in communications. I'm afraid he's somehow gotten the idea that you're not planning to accept his offer. I've been wanting to talk to him in person to clear things up, but I've been tied up in court the past few weeks, and when I was available, he didn't seem to be."

"I'm sure it will eventually get straightened out," Serena replied. If Mitch hadn't been so high-handed, she'd have told him herself that she simply wanted to spend some time at the ranch before signing it away. But after his arrogant attitude, she'd leave it to Mr. Hubbard to make the explanations. She wanted as little to do with Mitch as possible.

While they were talking, Hubbard had been arranging the documents on his desk into a neat pile. "I'm just going to give these to my secretary," he explained. Excusing himself, he stepped through the doorway. "Will you take care of these papers please, Rosemary?" she heard him say to the older woman who presided over his outer office.

His return was interrupted by the sound of the door to the street opening. He stopped in the doorway between the two offices and glanced back to see who was coming in. "Speak of the devil," he said with a grin. "Just the man I've been wanting to see. You're a hard man to reach, Mitch Tanner."

"Sorry you haven't been able to get in touch with

me, Ralph.'' Mitch's deep voice was clearly audible through the open door. ''I've been busy meeting with some out-of-town cattle buyers. I had to come into Cougar Bluff today, so I thought I'd drop by and give you a message to pass on to the new owner of the Double C.''

''Why don't you tell her yourself?'' Hubbard suggested. ''She's—''

''If you don't mind, I'd rather not have any more to do with that muleheaded, bad-tempered woman than I have to.''

Serena felt her anger rising. So he considered her muleheaded and bad-tempered, did he? Boy, if *that* wasn't a classic case of the pot calling the kettle black!

''Just tell her I'm ready to raise my offer, even though I think it's highway robbery.''

The corners of the lawyer's mouth twitched, as if he were trying hard to suppress his amusement. ''Ah—Mitch, there's something you should know—''

Serena rose and came to stand next to Mr. Hubbard in the doorway. ''You don't have to raise the price,'' she said to Mitch. ''Your original offer was satisfactory. I'll leave you and Mr. Hubbard to work out the details of the sale. Good day.'' With this she swept out of the office, past an open-mouthed Mitch and an amused Rosemary.

In spite of her cool demeanor, her heart was thudding as she hurried down the street. It wasn't until she'd walked the two blocks to where she'd parked that the high color in her cheeks began to subside.

* * *

Serena was halfway home when strange sounds began to emanate from beneath the hood of the pickup. She wasn't sure whether to continue on her way or pull over and—and what? Not being of a mechanical turn of mind, she had no idea what might happen if she continued to drive a vehicle that obviously had something wrong with it. Would that make the problem worse? On the other hand, if she stopped, what would she be able to do? While she was pondering this, the decision was taken out of her hands as the pickup lost power, then quietly died.

After she had steered toward the shoulder and coasted to a stop, she simply sat in stunned dismay for several seconds. Then, operating on the theory that any kind of activity was preferable to sitting around doing nothing, she got out and lifted the hood of the truck. She wasn't sure what she expected to find—a loose wire, perhaps, or something else that she could tighten or reconnect so she could be on her way.

But as she peered at the jumble of unfamiliar parts, she couldn't spot anything noticeably amiss. With a resigned sigh she climbed back into the truck, leaving the hood up so anyone who came by would know she was having trouble and hadn't stopped just to admire the view.

As she surveyed her predicament, she realized she was in for a long wait. She wasn't likely to be missed at the ranch for several hours. Farley and Homer would be so busy with their duties that it would be a while before they noticed she hadn't returned.

From her position atop a small rise, where she could

see for miles in either direction, it was obvious that walking either to the ranch or back to town was out of the question. And setting out across the open countryside would be risky. She had no choice but to sit and wait for someone to come along.

As the minutes stretched into an hour, she had ample time to go over in her mind the scene in Ralph Hubbard's office. She had already found out, from Farley, that Mitch was sole owner of the highly prosperous Diamond T Ranch. The old cowhand was as garrulous as Homer was taciturn and delighted in sharing his vast store of knowledge on the area and its inhabitants. She had only to introduce a subject, and he could go on at length. She had gleaned many bits of useful and interesting information from his discourses.

In this instance she had casually remarked to Farley that Mitch seemed rather young to own such a large piece of property.

"Inherited it from his uncle," Farley had replied. "His folks died when he was young, and his pa's older brother Frank took him in. Treated him just like a son. When the old man died, he left the place to Mitch, lock, stock, and barrel."

Serena pondered this information now. Apparently Mitch felt that his inherited wealth entitled him to whatever he wanted. After watching him free a calf from a mudhole, she had been willing to admit she might have misjudged him, that anyone who could be so gentle with a frightened baby animal *had* to have some good points. But when he'd charged into Hubbard's office today and accused her of being muleheaded and bad-tempered, she'd decided her original assessment of him had been correct. She burned with resentment at the memory. What right did he have to make judgments, anyway? He knew nothing of her reasons for not wanting to sell the ranch right away.

For a while her righteous indignation helped make the time pass more quickly, and she entertained herself by thinking up scathing replies to Mitch's next verbal attack. After almost two hours even that pastime began to pall, however, and she almost cheered when she spotted a small dot in the rearview mirror, moving toward her.

But her relief was short-lived. As the dot came closer and began to take on form and color, she could make out the boxy shape of a Blazer—a blue one.

By the time Mitch pulled over and braked to a stop just behind the pickup, Serena had had time to compose herself. With as much dignity as she could muster, she got out of the truck. In spite of herself, she couldn't suppress the feeling that everything was going to be all right now. No matter how she felt about the man personally, there was no denying he exuded a reassuring air of having everything under control.

To his credit, Mitch didn't ask pointless questions, such as, *Are you having car trouble?* With a curt nod in Serena's direction, he strode to the front of the disabled vehicle. His brow furrowed in concentration as he peered under the open hood.

Unsure of what was expected of her, Serena hovered at his elbow. "It has a new distributor cap," she offered in an attempt to be helpful.

He barely acknowledged this information as he jiggled a wire or two tentatively and tested some connections. "Get in the truck," he directed without looking at her. "I'll tell you when to start the ignition."

Once she was behind the steering wheel, she couldn't see what Mitch was doing, but after a few minutes he called, "Okay, start 'er up." She did as he asked, but when the truck failed to start after several tries, Mitch waved his arm for her to stop. Serena felt vaguely guilty, as if she were somehow at fault.

After this performance had been repeated three or four times, Mitch closed the hood and wiped his hands on his jeans. "I think you need a new coil," he said. "We'll have to leave the truck here for now. Come on, I'll give you a lift to the ranch." He opened the door for her.

For just a second Serena considered refusing his offer, until she recalled what her options were. Unless she wanted to sit here all day, waiting for someone else to come along, she was going to have to swallow her pride. "Thank you," she murmured. But she hesitated as she was about to get into the Blazer.

"Something wrong?"

She looked back at the pickup truck uncertainly. "Shouldn't I lock up?"

"Are you worried that somebody will steal it?" Mitch asked in a dry tone.

She had to admit, he had a point. Even if someone could get it started, who in his right mind would want it? With a little shrug, she turned her back on the disabled vehicle and climbed into the Blazer. She thought she'd detected a note of humor in Mitch's voice when he'd made that last comment, but a glance in his direction convinced her she'd imagined it. His profile had lost none of its granitelike hardness as he put the Blazer into gear and pulled out around the pickup.

They rode along for several minutes without speaking. Mitch was the first to break the silence. "After you stormed out of Ralph's office this morning—"

"I didn't 'storm' out."

"Okay, after you—ah—left rather hurriedly," he amended, a touch of sarcasm in his voice, "Ralph explained that you were planning to accept my offer on the ranch. Wouldn't it have simplified things if you'd just told me that in the first place? Why did you let me go on thinking you didn't intend to sell or were holding out for a better offer?"

Serena considered this, then countered with a question of her own. "Why didn't you tell me, that day you gave me a lift from the airport, that you were the one who wanted to buy the ranch?"

"I suppose because I was still angry at finding out my offer had been turned down."

"But I didn't turn it down," Serena pointed out. "It wasn't *my* fault if you jumped to the mistaken conclusion that my only interest in the Double C was in how big a profit I could make."

"What else could I think? As long as you were planning to go through with the sale, anyway, it would have saved everyone a lot of trouble if you'd just gone ahead and signed the papers in the first place."

"I—I just wanted to see the ranch before selling it.

It didn't seem that it would be a good business practice to sign away a piece of property without at least looking it over first.''

''Why?'' he challenged. ''Did you think Ralph and I were trying to put something over on you?''

A flash of anger surged through her. So he was going to turn the tables and put *her* in the wrong! Well, two could play that game. ''As long as we're throwing accusations around, why *are* you so anxious to buy the Double C?'' she countered.

He hesitated before replying, as if choosing his words carefully. ''If you're so concerned about 'good business practices,' have you considered what's going to happen to the ranch if it's allowed to go very long without the proper management? I watched your father struggle for years to make a go of the place. I don't want to see all his hard work go down the drain.''

''And you're quite sure that will happen if I'm allowed to have anything to do with running the Double C, even for a few weeks?''

''Well?'' He managed to turn the one word into an accusation. ''Don't try to pretend you know anything about ranching. I knew your father for years, and not once did you ever show any interest in the ranch—or in *him,* for that matter.''

All at once Serena felt her anger draining away, to be replaced by a dull, heavy sadness. ''If you knew my father so well, then you're probably aware that my parents separated before I was born,'' she said quietly. ''He never initiated any personal contact. What was I supposed to do?''

"You could have. . . ." His voice trailed off, as if he weren't sure exactly *what* she should have done. He glanced over at her curiously, almost as though he were trying to decide if the wistful note she hadn't been able to keep from her voice were real or merely a ploy to gain his sympathy.

Serena opened her mouth to say something in her defense, then closed it again. She'd almost revealed to him why it was so important to her to spend some time at the ranch before irrevocably signing it away. She decided, however, that she would rather let Mitch go on misunderstanding her motives than expose her inner feelings to him. She had already come perilously close to allowing him a glimpse of her deeper emotions.

Anyway, he had made up his mind about her, she reminded herself, and he wasn't likely to give up his preconceived ideas. She lapsed into silence, and they rode the rest of the way to the ranch without speaking.

Farley glanced out of the barn when the Blazer pulled into the driveway. He obviously guessed what must have happened when he spotted Serena in the passenger seat, and his expression was a mixture of relief and dismay. "I was just thinking about coming to look for you in the Jeep," he said as he opened the door for her. "I'm sure sorry, ma'am. I should never have let you drive that ol' wreck into town."

"It wasn't your fault. You warned me it wasn't running right," she reminded him.

"We left it about five miles from here," Mitch put in. "I think it needs a new coil."

With a brief thank-you to Mitch, Serena left him discussing truck repairs with Farley as she hurried into the house. She'd had enough of his company for one day.

# *Chapter Six*

The soft, almost plaintive nickering sound lingered in Serena's consciousness even after the wispy dream fragments had drifted away.

She found herself wide-awake, staring into the darkness. A glance at the digital travel clock on the nightstand told her it was just past three A.M. She sat up in bed, listening for—she wasn't sure what. Only the normal night sounds came to her.

*Had* she been awakened by a horse's whinny? She wondered if she ought to go down to the barn just to make sure Lady, the quarter horse mare, was all right. She told herself, however, that it wasn't necessary. Farley's trailer was close to the barn, and if Lady so much as hiccupped, he would be at her side in minutes. He would know exactly what to do for her, and Serena would only be in the way.

But then she recalled, with a sinking feeling, that Farley wasn't there. He'd taken a few much-needed days off to tend to some personal business and would be gone overnight. ''Lady ain't due to foal for a week or two, so I better get all this stuff done now,'' he'd said. ''You shouldn't have no problems while I'm gone. Homer'll be here during the day.''

That was no help to her now, however, in the wee hours of the morning. It was a little intimidating to realize *she* was the one in charge. She had a sudden urge to go check on Lady, just to ease her mind. But that was ridiculous, she told herself. If her imagination was playing tricks on her and the mare was dozing peacefully, she would probably cause more problems than she'd solve by going into the barn in the middle of the night and disturbing the animals.

She lay back down and closed her eyes, but sleep eluded her. She kept hearing Farley's gravelly voice telling her how her father had counted on the sale of Lady's foal to bring some much-needed working capital to the Double C.

'' 'Course, it don't matter now—the money, I mean,'' he'd said. ''When Mitch takes over, he won't have to pinch pennies the way your pa did. Still, it'd be a shame if anything went wrong. Lady's a fine mare, and she's been bred to one of the best quarter horse studs in the county.''

Finally Serena sat up and pushed back the covers. With a resigned sigh she slipped out of bed and pulled on jeans and a heavy sweater. *Better safe than sorry,* she thought, recalling one of her grandmother's favorite axioms.

When she entered the barn, she found Lady breathing heavily and shifting her weight from side to side. At the first sight of Serena she whinnied nervously and rolled her eyes, but she seemed to relax somewhat when Serena entered the box stall and began talking softly to her.

Even to Serena's inexperienced eye, it was obvious that Lady's time was close. She felt a shiver of apprehension at the realization that Farley wasn't here to take charge, but then she reminded herself that animals gave birth all the time without assistance. It was unlikely that anything would go wrong.

Although going back to bed and letting nature take its course seemed the wisest course of action, Serena couldn't bring herself to do that. She'd have felt as if she were deserting a sinking ship. Besides, even though there was nothing she could do to help, her presence seemed to calm the mare. She sat down in the straw just outside the stall, with her back against the rough boards, to await further developments.

She dozed off, and when she awoke, Lady was pacing the box stall, stopping every now and then to toss her head. Her eyes seemed glazed, and her coat was shiny with sweat.

A ripple of fear ran through Serena as she realized Lady was in real distress now. How she wished Farley were here, but she had no idea how to get in touch with him. What would happen to the mare—and her foal—if some kind of assistance wasn't forthcoming soon? Suddenly the financial loss to the ranch took secondary importance to the thought of letting this beautiful animal suffer and perhaps die.

Serena's initial panic began to subside as she forced herself to look at the problem rationally. *Homer, of course*. If Farley couldn't be reached, Homer was the next logical person to call on.

"Hang on, girl," she whispered just before dashing toward the house. "I'll get you some help."

But she couldn't find a Homer McCall in the dog-eared telephone book, and a call to Directory Assistance informed her that there was no listing for anyone with that name. Somehow this came as no surprise to Serena. It was in keeping with his character that the crusty old cowhand wouldn't be bothered with such modern foolishness as a telephone.

She glanced about the kitchen, as if expecting to spot some answer to her dilemma. And there it was, right in front of her—the business card taped to the wall just above the telephone. She'd noticed it before, of course, but until now she had had no reason to pay any attention to it. *Howard Blakely, D.V.M.*, it read, and she'd heard Farley mention "Doc Blakely, the vet. . . ." Giving a sigh of relief, she dialed the number. In a few minutes the vet would be on his way and the matter would be out of her hands.

But the doctor was already out on a call, his wife told Serena apologetically. "I can send him over as soon as he comes back," she offered, "but he'll likely be out for quite a while longer. I'll have him call you when he gets in."

Surely there had to be more than one animal doctor in a ranching community such as Cougar Bluff. With trembling fingers Serena riffled through the yellow pages of the telephone book until she found *Veteri-*

*narians*. Three were listed, including one whose advertisement read, *Practice limited to small animals*.

Of the remaining two, she tried the first one and was told that he was unavailable. It seemed that someone's prize bull had suffered severe cuts when he'd blundered into some barbed wire. The next doctor was also occupied. Something about an animal with a broken leg. There had apparently been a rash of middle-of-the-night mishaps and ailments, keeping all the available veterinarians busy.

Serena felt ready to cry as she hung up the telephone. The only other person she could think of to call was—Mitch Tanner. He was a rancher; he'd know what to do. But, recalling their previous meetings, she shrank from asking him for help—until she remembered the frightened, distressed mare in the barn. Regardless of how she felt about Mitch, she couldn't let that beautiful animal suffer. She opened the telephone book again and scanned the T's until she came to *Tanner, M., Diamond T Ranch*.

"Hello." Mitch's voice, when it came over the line, sounded muffled and irritable. For just a second Serena was tempted to hang up before he discovered she was the one who had awakened him. What had made her think that he'd come, anyway, or that she had the right to ask him? But he might at least be able to supply the name of another vet, she reminded herself.

"Mitch, this is Serena Cole, at the Double C," she began, trying to control the shakiness in her voice. "I think my mare, Lady, is about to foal, and she seems to be having some trouble. Farley isn't here, and I can't get hold of Homer—''

''Have you called the vet? Your father always used Doc Blakely.''

''I tried, but he's out on a call. None of the vets in the phone book were available.''

For several seconds there was only silence on the other end of the line. Then he said, ''I'll be right over.''

She hurried back out to the barn to stay with Lady while she waited for Mitch. Although the mare was lying down in the stall now, her distress didn't seem to have eased, and Serena felt more and more helpless. She was almost in tears by the time she heard wheels on the gravel driveway. Mitch was already rolling up his sleeves as he came into the barn.

''Thank you so much—'' Serena began, hurrying to meet him.

He brushed past her with a brief nod, his attention focused on the mare. ''It's a good thing you called me,'' he said after a quick but obviously knowledgeable appraisal of the situation. ''The foal seems to be in the wrong position, but I think we can save it.''

That ''we'' had a comforting sound. Serena felt as if a heavy load had been lifted from her shoulders.

''I'm going to need your help,'' Mitch went on. ''Can I depend on you to not get squeamish on me?''

''I'll do whatever you ask,'' she replied.

''Good. Let's get down to business then. First, would you bring a pail or basin of hot water and lots of towels? Then we'll need soap, antiseptic, and iodine.

You'll probably find most of those things in the tack shed. I imagine Farley already has them on hand."

When she returned with the asked-for items, Mitch was kneeling beside Lady, murmuring comforting words to her. Without looking up, he nodded for Serena to take a position by the mare's head.

"I can see its hooves," he said. "I was right—it's going to be a breech birth."

"What can I do to help?"

"For now, just hold her head—try to keep her still."

He got up long enough to pour a little of the antiseptic into the hot water and wash his hands and arms thoroughly. Then he returned to the mare's side and continued his ministrations. Every so often he would give an instruction to Serena, in a voice of quiet authority.

She had no trouble following his clear, easy-to-understand directions, and before long she almost seemed to anticipate his needs. Occasionally he'd say encouragingly, "You're doing just fine." As they worked together in the shadowy half light of the barn, Serena forgot her dislike of this man. For the time being, they weren't enemies; they were simply two people struggling together to accomplish a goal.

The first faint streaks of pink were barely visible in the sky when the foal—a colt—finally emerged. Apprehension lay like an icy ball in the pit of Serena's stomach as she regarded the limp, unmoving form. "Is it—?" She couldn't bring herself to voice her fears.

With infinite tenderness Mitch wiped the infant's nose and mouth, and it drew its first shaky breath. "He should be all right now," he said.

Serena went almost limp with relief.

She watched with interest as Mitch toweled the damp, shivering animal dry and treated its navel stub with iodine. She couldn't help but notice how gentle his strong, firm hands were as he tended the tiny creature.

Lady seemed too spent to show any interest in her offspring until Mitch carefully pushed him up against his mother. Then the transformation was remarkable. Her ears came forward, and a sparkle replaced the dull, empty look in her eyes. Instinctively she began to wash him with her rough tongue.

Serena felt as if she had participated in a miracle. Maybe it was because she was so moved by what she was seeing, or perhaps it was simply that her thinking was befuddled from having been up half the night, but all at once her normal reserve deserted her. In a burst of pure, spontaneous joy, she engulfed Mitch in an enthusiastic and heartfelt hug. He responded instinctively, by bringing his own arms up around her. For a few seconds they were simply two people who had shared a deep emotional experience.

As she heard Mitch's heart beating against her ear, Serena suddenly became aware of the way his lean, muscular body was pressed close to hers. She was caught completely off guard by the wave of unexpected emotions that rippled through her. At that moment Mitch's embrace tightened, almost imperceptibly, but enough to tell her that the sudden attraction wasn't altogether one-sided. She had to stifle a little gasp as every cell and nerve end in her body seemed to leap to sudden life.

This would never do, of course. She twisted her head around so that she was looking up at him. "You can . . ." she began, but her words trailed off weakly as she realized that his lips were just inches from hers. A slight movement was all it would take. . . .

She drew a shaky breath. With a real effort of will, she forced her wildly spinning emotions back under control and tried again. "You can let go of me now." Although she was striving for a light tone, her voice sounded strange and unnatural.

"Oh—sure. Sorry." But Mitch made no move to comply. In fact, he hardly seemed aware that he was still holding her. Then, as if he were suddenly coming back to reality, he dropped his arms so hastily that Serena almost lost her balance.

She drew back until there was a discreet foot or two between them. "I—I'm sorry. I didn't mean to throw myself at you that way. It's just that—I guess I got carried away. I mean—I was so worried about Lady—and I've never assisted at a foaling before—" Good heavens, she was babbling like an idiot, she realized.

"I understand," he said, smiling. "I've assisted at quite a few ranch births, but the sense of wonder never goes away."

Suddenly Serena found herself relaxing and her embarrassment slipping away. When he smiled that way, he didn't seem nearly as forbidding and intimidating. And she sensed that he really *did* share her feelings about the miracle they had just witnessed.

"Is there anything else I need to do for Lady?" she asked.

"You can give her a drink of lukewarm water every so often, but other than that I think we can pretty much depend on nature to take over from here." He fell into step beside her as they left the barn together.

As they came out into the sunlight, it occurred to Serena that after he'd gotten out of bed in the middle of the night to answer her plea for help, she owed him *something*. "Would you like to come in and have some breakfast?" she asked. "You've earned it."

When he didn't reply right away, Serena found herself wishing she could take back her impulsive invitation. Why hadn't she kept still? First she'd thrown herself into his arms, and now here she was practically *chasing* him, or so it must seem to him.

But surprisingly, he said, "That sounds great. I could use some breakfast."

Mitch made quick work of the bacon, eggs, and toast Serena cooked. She couldn't help thinking how relaxed and at-home he seemed, sitting across from her. But then, he'd probably spent more time in this kitchen than she had, she reminded herself. He and her father had been friends as well as neighbors.

Serena had worried that once the initial excitement of the colt's birth had abated, they might not be able to think of a thing to say to each other. She'd had a sudden vision of the two of them sitting across from each other at the table in uncomfortable silence. However, she needn't have worried. Conversation flowed easily. It was as if they had reached an unspoken agreement to put aside their former antagonism, at least for the time being. It all seemed so petty, anyway, after the experience they had just shared.

"How do you happen to know so much about horses?" Serena asked as they lingered over coffee. "You seemed to know exactly what to do for Lady."

Mitch appeared to be thinking this over. "It must be my Native American heritage," he replied after a pause.

Serena couldn't tell whether or not he was teasing her. "Your—ah—Native American heritage," she echoed.

"One of my forebears, way back in the family tree, was a Nez Percé Indian. I figured it out once, and I think I'm something like one-sixteenth or one-thirty-second Native American," he explained with a grin.

Nez Percé. Serena searched through her mental store of half-forgotten information. "Wasn't that the tribe that eluded soldiers for several months to avoid being moved from their homeland and taken to a reservation?" It was coming back to her now, from junior-high American History.

She recalled how tears had come to her eyes as she'd read about Chief Joseph's "I will fight no more forever" speech. How did it go? There was something about, ". . . no blankets, no food . . . the little children are freezing to death . . . I am tired; my heart is sick and sad. . . ." Even now, just thinking about it brought a lump to her throat.

She found herself looking at Mitch in a different way. She wondered if that small bit of Indian ancestry he could lay claim to accounted for his high cheekbones, ramrod-straight carriage, and almost black hair. Then she chided herself for being fanciful. That one-thirty-second was hardly enough to be counted—unless it was an exceptionally strong gene that had been passed down through several generations. Still, there was *something* that set him apart, that made him different from the other men of her acquaintance.

"To answer your original question, the Nez Percé were noted for their skill with horses," Mitch said, breaking into her thoughts. "I'd like to think I inherited the best traits of that unknown ancestor. They developed the breed called the Appaloosa, you know."

"The Appaloosa—aren't they those beautiful spotted horses?"

He nodded. "They were descended from Spanish horses, but the Nez Percé improved them by selective breeding."

"You must be very proud of your Nez Percé ancestry," she commented.

He shrugged. "Around here a good many people can claim a connection with some Indian tribe."

She felt slightly deflated to learn that something she found utterly fascinating was so matter-of-fact to him.

"Well, I did really get into Indian lore when I was a kid," he admitted, as if reading her thoughts. "When I first found out I had a Nez Percé ancestor, I started reading everything I could get my hands on about the tribe. I even went on a vision quest."

"A vision quest?" Although she wasn't sure what that was, it sounded interesting.

"It was sort of a ritual of growing up," he explained.

"It was observed by many tribes, not just the Nez Percé. Before becoming an adult, a young person would go out into the wilderness alone to fast and seek a special guardian—the Nez Percé word is *Weyekin*. This guardian spirit would take the form of some kind of animal or bird, and from then on would guard that person from danger. When I first read about the custom, I wanted to go on my own vision quest. I was young and impressionable—maybe twelve or thirteen—and I fancied myself a warrior."

His words evoked for Serena a mental picture of a boyish Mitch, already independent and self-reliant, poised on the brink of manhood.

"I didn't tell my uncle what I was planning to do," he went on. "I just asked if I could go out camping for a few days. If he suspected what I had in mind, he didn't try to talk me out of it."

"And did you find your guardian spirit?" Serena asked, eager to hear the rest of the story.

He grinned sheepishly. "Well, I'm not sure. I'd taken food along, to keep up the pretense that I was just going camping, but I didn't eat anything for the first few days. Fasting was part of the ritual. Now keep in mind, I was a normal boy with a healthy appetite. After a couple of days without food, my thinking was becoming a little fuzzy. I wasn't sure what was real and what wasn't. Even the rocks and trees were taking on strange characteristics."

The coffee in front of Serena was forgotten as she listened, completely absorbed.

"When I woke up on the third morning, I was so

weak and hungry, I was about to give it all up. I just lay there feeling like a failure, because my 'great experience' had fizzled out. Then when I opened my eyes, I saw this bird—it was a peregrine falcon—overhead."

"I thought peregrine falcons were kind of scarce."

"They were, even back then. Between the widespread use of DDT and the move during World War Two to eradicate them—because they were preying on homing pigeons, which were used as a means of communication—their numbers were already reduced. Even in this area they're rare. Not many people are fortunate to get a look at one.

"But there it was, outlined against the morning sky, making these big, lazy circles, and it moved lower and lower with each revolution. It seemed that it was almost close enough for me to reach out and touch it. Of course, that part was just an optical illusion, but I *did* see the peregrine. It was so beautiful—so strong and graceful—I felt then that I'd found my *Weyekin*."

Serena felt very close to Mitch, because he'd shared something of himself with her. She kept her thoughts to herself, however, reluctant to break the spell.

But Mitch broke it himself. "As I said, I was young and impressionable then, and I was convinced the peregrine had come just to reassure and strengthen me. I realize now, of course, that there was nothing supernatural about the sighting." He hesitated, as if unsure whether to go on. Then, with a self-conscious smile, he admitted, "Still, to this day I've felt an affinity for the peregrine falcon."

Serena recalled the bird she'd spotted the first time

she'd gone out riding. Even from a distance she'd sensed the enormous power in that relatively small body. She was about to ask Mitch if it could possibly have been a peregrine, when he glanced at his watch and said, "Hey, I'd better get back. Since I left in the middle of the night, I didn't tell anyone where I was going. I'll probably get a good scolding from Cloris for not leaving word."

Serena fought to control a raising of her eyebrows. She told herself firmly that it didn't matter to her in the least that some woman named Cloris had the right to keep tabs on his whereabouts.

Still, she couldn't suppress a stab of relief when Mitch explained, "Cloris is my housekeeper. She fusses over me like a mother hen."

They made light conversation as Serena accompanied him outside. Walking along side by side, their arms occasionally brushed, and her skin tingled from the slight contact. She glanced down in surprise, almost expecting to see sparks of electricity flowing between them.

When they reached the Blazer, Serena turned to Mitch, tilting her face up to his. She had intended to thank him for his help, but her words were forgotten as her eyes met his. An explosive current seemed to leap across the small space that separated them, bringing to mind the few seconds she'd spent in his arms earlier this morning.

Although common sense told her that her wisest course of action would be to step back from him before she lost her head again, she couldn't seem to make her limbs obey. His nearness radiated a magnetism that drew her into it, that sapped her strength and her will. The intoxicating warmth that was permeating every fiber of her being left her weak and trembling.

Something intense flared up in her as her instincts told her he wanted to—*intended* to—kiss her. With a feeling that there was no sense in trying to escape the inevitable—not that she even wanted to—she simply waited. Already she could almost feel the pressure of his lips. His eyes still held hers. They were like dark pools, and she was being pulled into them. . . .

All at once his glance focused on something beyond her. The brief pause brought her abruptly back to reality. As she gathered the shreds of her self-control around her like a protective garment, she turned to find out what had claimed Mitch's attention. Homer's Jeep was just turning into the driveway. Ordinarily it could be heard from a good distance away, but she had to admit her thoughts had been otherwise occupied.

Self-consciously Serena took a step backward as she and Mitch watched Homer head for his usual parking spot near the barn. "I—I'd better go tell him about the new arrival," she said, trying to restore some semblance of normalcy to the situation. She couldn't control the shakiness in her voice, however. "He'll be disappointed that he missed the main event." Relieved to have something to focus her attention on, she hurried off toward Homer.

She glanced over her shoulder once and saw Mitch still standing there watching her, but a few seconds later she heard the Blazer's engine come to life.

## *Chapter Seven*

"Serena!" Kelly's voice came over the line. "Thank goodness I finally caught you. I've been trying to reach you for days, but I guess every time I called, you were out rounding up cows or whatever it is you're doing out there."

Serena couldn't help being amused at her friend's implication that whatever news she had to impart was so earthshaking it couldn't wait. After all, they had just had a long telephone conversation last week. But with Kelly, *everything*, from a broken fingernail to finding *two* prizes in her box of Cracker Jack, was a major event. That was one of the reasons the two young women were such good friends. Kelly's irrepressible enthusiasm was the perfect complement to Serena's unruffled calmness.

"Kelly, it's great to hear from you," she said. "What's new?"

"What's new!" Kelly echoed. "So much has been happening, I hardly know where to begin. The company Russell works for—DynaTec—is sending him to

Germany as part of a team that's updating a computer system for a manufacturing plant over there. He has to be there in a few weeks, and the project will probably take at least a year. It's a wonderful opportunity for him—just the break he needs to really demonstrate what he can do!''

Obviously this was one time when Kelly's excitement was justified. The Russell she was referring to was Russell Hall, a systems analyst with a computer firm. He and Kelly had recently become engaged and were planning to marry in the fall. Serena wondered what effect this new development would have on their wedding plans.

Kelly's next words answered that question. ''He wants me to go with him, of course, which means we'll have to move up our wedding. There isn't time for anything except the simplest type of ceremony, so we're being married this weekend. I wish we could wait until you get back, but there's so much to be done before we leave, this is the only time we can fit it in. The trip to Germany will be our honeymoon.''

When Kelly finally paused for breath, Serena had time to digest all this information. As she sorted out the details of Kelly's rapid, nonstop monologue, she had to blink back tears. Her closest friend was getting married and moving halfway around the world, and she wouldn't even be able to attend the wedding.

''How wonderful for both of you! I'm sure this will give Russell's career just the boost it needs. And I envy you, getting to travel overseas.'' Although Serena tried to put the proper enthusiasm into her voice, inside she felt empty. Oh, she was pleased that Kelly was marrying the man she loved and embarking on an interesting adventure, but she was certainly going to miss her longtime friend. Since junior high school, they had shared confidences, hopes and dreams for the future, successes and disappointments. . . .

She tried to concentrate on the rest of what Kelly was saying. "Since I'll be on my way to Germany by the time you get back, I have to know what you want me to do about the apartment. I'm really sorry to leave you stuck with the rent on a two-bedroom place, but in view of the letter I—we—just received—it was addressed to *both* of us, of course, but I went ahead and opened it—I guess it really doesn't make much difference—about the apartment, I mean, since we'd have to move out when our lease expires in two months, anyway. . . ."

What in the world was Kelly going on about? Serena wondered. What did she mean about having to move out? Naturally they'd been planning to renew their lease. *For heaven's sake, get to the point,* she thought. Sometimes her friend's habit of rambling was frustrating.

"Oh, yes, the letter," Kelly went on, as if she knew exactly at what point Serena's patience would start to wear thin. "It came yesterday, and it said the building has been sold and will be demolished to make room for a new shopping center as soon as all existing leases have expired. Oh, and 'for the tenants' convenience, any who desire to terminate their leases early may do so.'

"So anyway, do you want to keep the apartment? I thought since the lease is almost up, maybe you'd rather just give it up now so you won't have to pay rent on it by yourself. If you'd like, I can pack up your things and store them in my folks' attic until you get back and find another place."

The unexpected loss of her home, combined with the sudden news of Kelly's impending departure, left Serena feeling forlorn and disconsolate. Not that the structure itself had any special significance—it was simply a basic apartment building, functional, but with little personality or character. She and Kelly had lived there only a year. Still, it was the only home she had, and now it was being taken from her.

She forced her practical side to take over. She would have to give up the apartment in a little over a month, anyway, when the lease expired. "Why don't you go ahead and move my things out?" she told Kelly. She didn't relish the idea of having to go apartment-hunting almost the minute she stepped off the plane, but since there wasn't much she could do about it now, she resolutely put the matter out of her mind for the time being.

"Now then," she said, "since I won't get to be there for your wedding, I at least want to hear all the details. What kind of dress are you wearing? And what about flowers? Oh—and pictures—be sure to send lots of pictures. . . ."

As Serena maneuvered Penny alongside the large rural mailbox so she could reach in without dismounting, she reflected on how even a matter as simple as "bringing in the mail" was more complicated here in this land of vast open spaces. Back home, she merely had to step out the front door. Here, unless she was in the mood for a long hike, it involved either getting into the truck and driving up to the main road, or saddling a horse and riding there.

She glanced through the stack of mail briefly before tucking it into the bag attached to her saddle and heading Penny back toward the house. Besides the usual assortment of bills and advertisements, there was a long, official-looking envelope bearing the imprint of the school district she would be teaching in.

On the ride back to the ranch she spotted a pair of young hawks off in the distance. By now she'd learned enough about the wildlife in the area that she was able to identify them as red-tailed hawks. "Kinda purty to watch, but not anything unusual," Farley had told her.

Still, the sight brought to mind Mitch's revelation about his vision quest and sighting the peregrine falcon. The knowledge that he'd felt close enough to her to share what must have been a very personal experience gave her a warm feeling. She was relieved that she and Mitch had been able to put aside their differences. She was an orderly, methodical person who liked loose ends neatly tied up. It went against all her principles to leave with an unresolved conflict between them, even though she knew she would never see him again once she went home.

He had dropped by several times since that morning when she'd helped him deliver Lady's foal, now named

Lucky. ''Have to see how the lil' feller's doing,'' he'd said.

The ''lil' feller'' was, in fact, doing fine. Serena and Mitch had stood with their arms hooked over the top rail of the fence, laughing at the antics of the wobbly-legged youngster. He would set off to explore his surroundings on his own, but any threat—real or imagined—was enough to send him back to the security of his mother's side.

Serena brushed aside any passing thought she'd had that Mitch might have come by expressly to see her. She reminded herself that he had a valid reason for wanting to check on the progress of the colt. As part of the ranch's livestock, Lucky would be included in the sale that would take place later today. She would be on her way back to Windham tomorrow, and Lucky would be Mitch's property.

Serena suppressed the pang of emptiness that suddenly took hold of her at the thought that once the papers were signed, she wouldn't be seeing Mitch again. Hadn't she already had this out with herself when she'd lain awake at night, unable to erase the memory of Mitch's arms around her and his lips close to hers?

She'd reminded herself that Windham was her home. Despite the fact that she was owner of the Double C, she was only a visitor here, an outsider. So what if she *was* physically attracted to Mitch? They lived in different worlds. For the rest of her life she would always have pleasant memories when she thought of him, but that was all he could ever be to her—a pleasant memory. This was what her mind told her. Convincing her heart, however, was another matter.

It was a relief when the ranch buildings came into view. The long ride back had given her too much time to think about Mitch.

Once Penny had been tended to—one thing Serena had learned was that on a ranch the animals' needs came first—she settled down to look over her mail.

*Probably a form letter,* she thought as she opened the envelope from the school district. Most likely it contained such commonplace information as employee benefits and district policies. As she withdrew the single sheet of paper and scanned it, several phrases seemed to leap out at her: . . . *regret to inform you . . . budget cuts . . . teaching and administration staff are being reduced. . . . must withdraw our offer of employment . . . regret any inconvenience this has caused you, and we wish you luck in finding employment elsewhere.*

Serena read the letter three times, to make sure she hadn't misunderstood. But there was no mistake. The teaching job she had been looking forward to would not be forthcoming. Could they do that? she wondered. Obviously they *could.* No contract had been signed yet, so she supposed it was legal and there was nothing she could do about it.

It took several minutes for the full significance of her situation to sink in. She had no job to go back to. She could continue substitute teaching, of course, but she'd counted on the security of a permanent position.

And she not only had no job waiting for her—she didn't even have a place to live!

One of these factors—the lack of either a job or an apartment—wouldn't have been a major problem by itself. However, the idea of arriving in town and having to immediately find a place to live, while simultaneously looking for a means of livelihood, was less than appealing.

She almost wished she hadn't told Kelly to go ahead and give up their apartment. Even though she would have had to bear the entire expense by herself, at least she'd have a home for the next month. But there was no sense in worrying about what was over and done with—she had to make some plans for her future.

So many thoughts were whirling through her head that she barely heard the insistent jangle of the telephone. It was on its fourth ring when she roused herself from her distracted state to pick it up and utter a preoccupied, "Hello."

"Serena, this is Ralph Hubbard. I just called to find out what time you'll be stopping by my office today."

"Today?" she echoed vaguely. The unexpected turn of events had driven all other matters from her mind.

"This is the day you were going to come in and sign the papers for the sale of the ranch," Ralph prompted.

"Oh. Of course." She forced her attention back to Ralph's question. "I—ah—" She paused, her mind racing ahead. With her mother and Gram gone, she no longer had any family in Windham. She didn't even have a best friend there, she thought bleakly. This very minute Kelly was on her way to Germany with her new husband.

Right now the Double C was all she had to hang on to, she realized. Without it she would be as directionless as a leaf being tossed in the wind. She was aware that, with her limited knowledge of ranching, she wouldn't be able keep the place indefinitely. Still, for the time being it represented home and security. It was a place where she could retreat until she had a chance to absorb these sudden changes in her life and decide on her next move.

"Serena?" Ralph's voice came over the line. "Are you still there?"

"Yes, I'm here."

"I thought maybe we'd been cut off. You are coming in today, aren't you?"

She hesitated a fraction of a second before replying, "I'm afraid not."

"If you wait until tomorrow, won't that be crowding things a bit for you? What time does your plane leave?"

"I—I'm not leaving tomorrow. I've decided to stay here for a while longer."

There was a pause on the other end of the line. Then, "Do you mind if I ask why?"

"I found out several days ago that I was losing my apartment. The building is being torn down," she explained haltingly. "And then today I received word that the teaching job I was counting on has been withdrawn because the school district is making budget cuts."

"Uh-huh." Ralph sounded as if he were stalling for

time while he digested this new development. "Does this mean you won't be selling the ranch?"

"I'm afraid so," she replied in a voice that betrayed her utter dejection. "Right now the Double C is the only home I have. The way things stand, I have nothing to go back to. I can't let the ranch go until I've had time to see what my options are. I need time to make some plans."

"I see." His tone indicated that he grasped her predicament and was trying to be understanding. "Do you have any idea of how long that may be?"

"No," she admitted. "I'll let you know as soon as I can."

There, it was done, she thought as she hung up. For the time being, at least, she had a home, a place she could use as a "base of operations" while she contacted rental agents, wrote letters to prospective employers, and sent out résumés. Then when she had a job interview or two scheduled, or at least a couple of good leads, and maybe a line on a suitable apartment, she would return to Windham. But in the meantime there wouldn't be such an urgency to make a hasty—and perhaps wrong—decision.

Farley and Homer would have to be told. Her staying here depended, a good deal, on them. She went out the back door in search of the two men. She found Homer in the barn mending a halter.

"Do you have any idea where Farley is?" she asked.

Before Homer could reply, the other half of her work crew stepped in. "Somebody lookin' for me?"

"I'm glad you're both here," she began without preamble. "I need to talk to you."

It was obvious, from her tone, that she had more than a casual chat in mind. The two men glanced at each other, then gave her their full attention.

"What are your plans when the Double C is sold?" she asked. "Do you have other jobs lined up yet?"

"Wal, ma'am, Mitch Tanner already said he'd want us to come to work for him when he buys the place," Farley explained. "We'd just keep on doing what we do now, but we'd be doing it for him."

She wasn't sure how to work up to this, so she decided to just plunge right in. "I've changed my mind about selling the ranch, at least for now. How would you feel about working for me?"

At their identical expressions of baffled surprise, she quickly explained about losing her apartment, as well as her prospective employment. "I—I don't know what to do next," she admitted in halting words. "I have nothing to go back to in Windham—no home, no job. If I sell the ranch, I won't have anything." Although she was trying to put forth her position in a straightforward manner, she couldn't keep her voice from breaking slightly.

"Once I've had time to get organized, I'll go ahead with the sale of the ranch, of course," she went on, "but in the meantime I don't see where I have any choice but to stay here. I'm asking you to stay on and help me keep things going. I realize you'll be short-handed—when my father was alive, there were three of you to do the work—but I'll do my share. You'll have to tell me what needs to be done, but I'll do whatever you say,'' she promised earnestly.

Farley rubbed his hand across his chin, as if he were deep in thought. It seemed an eternity before he spoke. Finally he said, ''Why, ma'am, I'd be proud to do whatever's necessary to help you stay on here. Charlie was a fine man and a good friend of mine, and I hate to see his place go to someone that ain't his kin. Much as I like and respect Mitch, I never cottoned to the idea of the Double C goin' out of the family, so to speak.''

Serena let her breath out in a sigh of relief. That was one hurdle she'd gotten over. She'd had a feeling she could count on Farley. Homer, however, was another matter. He hid his feelings behind a taciturn mask, so that she was never sure just what he was thinking. She glanced over at him questioningly.

''Me'n Farley been workin' together for a long time,'' he said. ''Don't know if I could get used to somebody new. If he's stayin', I guess that means I gotta stay too.''

Although his response was less than enthusiastic, at least he wasn't going to desert her.

''Thank you—both of you,'' she said. ''I can't tell you how much I appreciate this.''

''Ah—one thing—'' Homer added. ''I think you oughta keep in mind that Mitch ain't likely to be too happy about this. Just thought I should mention that.''

That possibility had already crossed her mind, of course. ''I guess that's a chance we'll have to take,'' she replied with a calmness she didn't feel.

Despite her show of confidence, she couldn't help

wondering just what Mitch *would* say when he found out she'd changed her mind about selling.

She didn't have to wait long to find out. She'd just reentered the house when she glanced out the window and saw his Blazer approaching at an alarming speed. It turned into the driveway and braked to a sudden stop. She winced and turned away as gravel went spewing out from beneath the tires. There was the sound of the car door slamming and, a few seconds later, heavy footsteps on the front porch.

She froze when she heard Mitch's determined, authoritative knock at the door. The thought of facing his wrath was so intimidating that for a brief second she seriously considered simply keeping quiet and pretending she wasn't home. Then her common sense took over. He wasn't going to be put off easily, so she might as well face up to him now and get it over with. Besides, it was ridiculous for her to be hiding from him as if she were some kind of criminal. There was no reason why they couldn't discuss this like civilized adults. He couldn't *force* her to sell, for goodness' sake.

Having given herself this little pep talk, she went to the door and opened it. Without waiting for an invitation, Mitch strode past her into the living room, while she watched with something close to alarm. Everything about him, from the thundercloud expression that darkened his features to the determined set of his shoulders, communicated his extreme disapproval.

"I—I see you've talked to Ralph Hubbard," she said.

He whirled around to face her. "You bet I did! I couldn't believe it when he said you were keeping the Double C. That has to be the stupidest decision anyone ever made."

Serena fought back the angry retort that sprang to her lips. "Didn't Ralph explain that I've lost my job and my apartment?"

"I don't see what that has to do with anything."

"You don't see— What do you expect me to do?" she demanded angrily. "Go back and wander around like a—a bag lady until I find a place to live and a job?"

"Don't overdramatize the situation. You must have some friends there you can stay with until you get organized."

"As a matter of fact, I can't think of anyone I'd impose on that way, except. . . ." Her voice trailed off as she recalled that her best friend was, at this very minute, on her way to Germany with her new husband. "Anyway, why should I have to go looking for someone to take me in when I can stay at *my* ranch?"

"You said you'd sell it to me," he reminded her. "We had a deal."

"No, we didn't. A 'deal' is an agreement between two people, not one person *browbeating* the other into giving in. *If* and *when* I decide to sell the Double C, I'll be glad to consider your offer, but you have no right to make me feel as if I'm somehow *obligated* to sell it to you. That's not my idea of a deal."

"Come on, Serena, you make it sound as if I'm the big, mean villain trying to cheat a poor little orphan out of the family farm. The main thing I'm concerned about is keeping you from making a total loss of everything your father struggled for just because you have a romanticized idea of what ranch life is all about. You don't know the first thing about raising cattle.''

''I realize that. But Homer and Farley have agreed to stay on. They have years of know-how and experience between them,'' she reminded him.

''I'm not putting down Homer and Farley. Nobody knows more about ranching than they do. But they're not getting any younger. Two old men can't run this whole spread.''

''When my father was alive, the three of them handled it,'' she pointed out. ''And, naturally, I don't intend to just sit back and watch them work. I plan to do my share.''

Mitch stood looking down at her. He lifted his hands as if he intended to place them on her shoulders, but then he dropped them and took a step backward. Serena wondered if he was afraid he might forget his arguments if he touched her. Recalling the attraction that had flowed between them that morning they'd delivered Lady's foal together, she decided that could be a very real possibility. For her own part, she knew that any physical contact was likely to make her lose track of anything she'd planned to say in her defense.

As if aware that his anger was accomplishing nothing, Mitch's tone changed to that irritatingly patient manner people use when trying to reason with a stubborn child. ''You aren't suited to ranch life. You're just not— Well, you're not tough enough.''

"Tough enough!" Serena echoed.

"I don't mean you're weak or afraid of hard work," he hastily amended. "What I'm trying to say is that you don't know what you're getting into. Even under the best of conditions, ranching is a hard, thankless job. It's getting up at the crack of dawn and slaving away until you think you're going to drop, and then somehow finding the strength to work some more. It's falling into bed so tired that every bone in your body aches. It's going out in the rain and snow, because the cattle have to be cared for even when the weather isn't to your liking."

"It was good enough for my father," Serena pointed out quietly. "Besides, when you consider that this is the only home I have now, that I have nothing to go back to, I don't see that I have much choice."

"I give up," Mitch said, raising his hands in a gesture of frustration. "I tried to talk some sense into you, but you won't listen to reason. You'll have to learn the hard way." Shaking his head, he turned and went out.

Once he was gone, Serena began to wonder if he might be right. Maybe she really didn't know what she was getting into. But right or wrong, the decision had been made and she had no intention of backing down now.

## *Chapter Eight*

There, that was the last section of fence to be repaired, Serena thought with relief. She put her tools in the truck bed, then reached around and rubbed the small of her back, trying to massage away the nagging ache that seemed to be a part of her these days.

Before getting back into the truck, she removed her wide-brimmed hat and wiped her forearm across her brow. She was beginning to realize that this form of headgear, almost part of a uniform around here, wasn't worn simply for looks. She was finding it indispensable for the shade it provided. She had also taken to wearing a large bandanna knotted loosely at her throat to protect the back of her neck from the sun.

She wished there were as easy a remedy for the weariness that consumed her. Until these past few weeks she hadn't known it was possible to be so incredibly tired or to hurt in so many different places.

Under Farley's and Homer's directions, she was learning to handle jobs that, until a little over a month ago, had been completely out of her sphere of experience. And the list of those jobs seemed endless. When she wasn't helping Farley make repairs on the barn and surrounding buildings, she was following Homer around the hay field, assisting him as he cleaned and checked the sprinkler system. By the time she finished removing the old, moldy hay from the barn so the new supply wouldn't be contaminated, it was time to clear brush from along the fenceline.

She had blisters on her hands from wielding unfamiliar tools, and she seemed to have developed a permanent crick in her back from the unaccustomed manual labor. There was a deep scratch just above one eye, where an overhanging branch had caught her unaware when she was flushing out cattle that had strayed too far from the rest of the herd. And she was still limping as a result of a face-to-face confrontation with an overprotective mama cow. She'd dismounted to extricate a calf from a tangle of barbed wire, and its mother had resented her efforts to be helpful. She'd twisted her ankle painfully while sidestepping the angry animal.

Farley had stifled an amused grin when she'd related the incident to him. But then he'd turned serious. "Take it easy," he'd advised, eyeing her with concern. "I know there's a lot to be done around here, but them cows ain't gonna die of neglect if it don't all get done right away. Ain't no need to work yourself to death."

But Serena was determined to keep her part of the bargain. She'd promised Farley and Homer that she'd do her share if they'd stay on and help keep the ranch going until she had time to make plans for her future.

She had no intention of going back on her word. She'd stick to her agreement if it killed her.

*And it just might,* she thought ruefully as she got into the truck and started it up. For the first time in her relatively sheltered life, her slender body was being pushed to its limits physically. More than once during these past few weeks it had occurred to her to wonder if she might have taken on more than she could handle. She pushed the thought aside, however. She was young and strong, and a little hard work wasn't going to do her any permanent harm.

As she maneuvered the pickup around rocks, brush, and other obstacles, she recalled, somewhat guiltily, that she wasn't any closer to settling her future. She still hadn't sent out any job résumés or contacted any rental agents. She had good intentions, but by the time all the ranch chores were finished each day, she was too tired to do anything but fall into bed.

She reminded herself that once the spring roundup—due to take place in a few weeks—was over, things would settle down a bit. She made up her mind to start making inquiries after the roundup.

Her attention was diverted by the sight of several cows up ahead, milling around and lowing mournfully. Since their behavior struck her as slightly out of the ordinary, she decided she'd better investigate. At her approach they slowly moved out of the way.

Even without getting out of the truck, she could see the reason for the reproachful looks they were giving her. The creek they were gathered around, which normally flowed with an abundance of clear, sparkling water, was now almost completely dried up. Only a thin stream of muddy liquid trickled over the rocks on the bottom.

Her mouth dropped open in dismay. Although this creek wasn't the Double C's sole source of water—there were the dams and irrigation ditches—it was the only water on this section of the ranch. Later in the summer it usually dried up, Farley had explained to her, but by that time the cattle had been moved to another spot. Even inexperienced as she was, she knew there was no reason for the creek to be dry this early in the year.

After braking to a stop and getting out, she followed the watercourse several hundred feet toward its source without finding the cause of the problem. *What could have happened*? she wondered. That creek meandered all over the Double C, making numerous twists and turns before it finally flowed into a small lake in a low section of the land. And it came from—

In her mind she pictured the map Ralph Hubbard had sent her. The creek flowed through Diamond T land before crossing the boundary onto the Double C. Could Mitch have somehow diverted the water before it reached her land? *Would* he have done such a thing? She wasn't sure just how far he would go to force her to give up and sell out to him.

Even if he *had* tampered with her water supply, where was all that water going? she wondered. Was it likely that he would flood his own land just to accomplish his purpose?

But a glance at the surrounding terrain told her there

wasn't much danger of that happening. She supposed the Diamond T was much like her own land, rough and uneven, with so many gullies and ravines that the stream could flow for miles in another direction without causing serious flooding.

It was hard to believe he'd do something so underhanded. He might be stubborn and overbearing, but outright sabotage hardly seemed his style. Yet if he was determined to make things as difficult as possible for her, what better way could he have found to do it than to obstruct her primary water source?

Well, he wasn't going to get away with it, she decided. If he thought he could make her knuckle under so easily, he had another think coming. That creek belonged to her too, and he had no right to tamper with it.

She whirled around and strode back to the truck, her entire being radiating righteous anger. With a squeal of tires she turned the vehicle around, then pressed her foot down hard on the accelerator. Bypassing the house and outbuildings, she headed across open country for the main road.

On Serena's trips into town she'd noticed the neatly lettered sign reading *DIAMOND T RANCH* that marked the entrance to Mitch's property. Now the old pickup swayed precariously as she slowed just enough to negotiate the turn onto the narrow, winding lane. Then the split-rail fences that bordered either side were flying past in a blur.

As she rounded the final curve, a large, solid-looking house came into view. Set well back among tall trees, it looked almost as if it were part of the landscape, with its touches of weathered stone across the front and its wide wooden beams. Although she had never seen Mitch's home before, she was too angry to pay much attention to its rustic charm now.

She came to such a screeching halt in front of the structure that several cowhands who were working in and around the nearby outbuildings glanced over at her curiously. She ignored them as she marched up to the front door and rapped sharply.

"It's open," a voice—Mitch's—called out.

Serena supposed that was an invitation to come in. He probably thought one of his employees had knocked. She hesitated, but only for a second. She didn't want to give her anger a chance to dissipate. Mindful of her mission here, she opened the door and stepped inside. She found herself in a wide entry hall.

Nobody seemed to be about. After looking around to get her bearings, she marched through the double doors in front of her. As she entered the large, high-ceilinged living room, she had a brief impression of natural wood paneling, furniture upholstered in earthy russets and browns, and deep, thick carpets. This was definitely a man's room. Everything about it exuded Mitch's presence.

As she stood wondering what to do next, a door opened and closed in another part of the house. She heard footsteps, and a few seconds later Mitch appeared from a hallway that opened into the room from the other side.

He was clad only in jeans and boots, and as he

entered, he was in the act of putting one arm through the sleeve of a shirt. His hair was damp, and a few drops of water glistened on his chest as if he had just recently showered. For a second or two Serena almost forgot the purpose of her visit. The sight of that muscular torso, tapering down to a flat abdomen and slim hips, was unsettling.

She faced Mitch with a determined air, forcing herself to ignore the emotions that were beginning to stir in her. She had serious business to settle with him, and she didn't intend to be deterred by the sight of a bare chest. Even so, she had time to admire the smooth, easy gait with which he moved before the sight of her brought him to a sudden halt.

The surprise on Mitch's face was almost comical. He was obviously caught off guard at finding himself face-to-face with Serena. His expression turned wary as he took in the granite hardness of her normally gentle blue eyes and the way her slender body almost quivered with indignation.

"I—ah—just got out of the shower," he explained when he found his voice, indicating the reason for his state of partial undress. "I've been out loading hay. That stuff is worse than itching powder. As you can see, I wasn't expecting company."

"You must have known I'd be paying you a visit. Surely you didn't think I was going to take this lying down. . . ."

Her voice faltered. She wished he'd finish dressing. That bare torso *was* distracting.

"Take what lying down?" he asked, in a tone that was a perfect blend of innocence and puzzled surprise.

Oh, he was putting on a good act, Serena thought. But she wasn't going to fall for it. "Just who do you think you are, tampering with my water supply?" she demanded. "I have as much right to that water as you. What am I supposed to do with all those thirsty cattle?"

"Serena, will you stop talking in riddles?" He shrugged into his shirt and fastened the snaps down the front as he approached her. "You come in here ranting and raving about water rights and thirsty cattle, and I have no idea what you're talking about."

Now he was standing directly in front of her, looking down at her. She found his nearness so unnerving that she instinctively took a step backward. She was determined not to be swayed from her reasons for confronting him.

"Drop the act," she snapped. "I know you were the one responsible for diverting that stream that runs through both of our ranches"—she paused for emphasis—"the stream that provides water for my livestock. I suppose you think if you make things difficult enough for me, I'll knuckle under. Well, if you believe I can be intimidated that easily, you're sadly mistaken. If it's a fight you want, that's what you'll get."

"Now let me get this straight." Slowly and methodically he rolled the cuffs of his sleeves back. "You're saying I somehow diverted your water supply—that you think I'd do something like that in order to force you to sell out?" Although his manner was calm and his voice controlled, there was something in his tone that sent a little shiver of apprehension through Serena.

She faced up to him without flinching, however. "That's exactly what I'm saying."

"I don't do things that way," he replied in clipped tones as he tucked his shirt into the waistband of his jeans.

"Then what happened to the creek?" she demanded.

"I don't know, but I intend to find out. Let's go."

He took Serena's arm and steered her toward the front door. She thought at first that his intention was to forcibly eject her from his home. Once they were outside, however, he guided her past her pickup truck to his Blazer.

She shrugged off his touch. "Just where do you think you're taking me?"

"I told you, to find out what happened to your water," he replied, opening the door for her. "Get in."

Although Serena's first impulse was to refuse, a quick glance at the determined set of his jaw convinced her that arguing with him while he was in this mood might not be wise. She got in without comment.

He put the Blazer in reverse and turned it around with quick, angry movements. Soon they were bouncing along a narrow, rutted dirt road that led to—who knew where? Serena's apprehension mounted as they got farther and farther away from the house. She had no idea where they were headed, and she wasn't sure if she liked the idea of being out here, so far from everything, with someone as angry as Mitch was right now.

Just as she was beginning to wonder if she'd made a serious mistake by not standing her ground and refusing to accompany him, he suddenly veered off to the right. He eased the Blazer around an outcropping of rock, then braked to a stop at the crest of a steep slope. He seemed to have completely forgotten Serena's presence. Without a glance in her direction, he got out and started down the slope, which was dotted with trees and brush. The vegetation grew thicker toward the bottom, and in seconds he was out of sight.

With a shrug Serena got out and followed him. She found him standing next to a stream, watching the clear, sparkling water gurgle by. His brow was wrinkled in concentration, and his expression was thoughtful.

"No problem here," he said when Serena joined him. "Come on, let's see if we can find out where the trouble is." He stepped aside to allow her to go ahead of him.

He seemed to have forgotten his icy resentment of a few moments ago. Now he appeared to be more concerned with getting to the bottom of the mystery than in defending himself against Serena's accusations. She wasn't sure how to take this change in his attitude. It could be a diversionary tactic to throw her off guard. Still, at this point she didn't see what choice she had but to go along with the pretense, if that's what it was. Warily she stepped past him.

"Careful, it's slippery along here," he cautioned,

indicating the muddy ground and moss-covered rocks at the edge of the stream. He put a hand under Serena's elbow to guide her past a spot that was particularly hard to negotiate.

Irritably Serena jerked her arm away. At that moment she stepped on wet rock, and her foot slipped out from under her. Instinctively Mitch reached out to keep her from falling.

As his arms closed around her, the sudden rush of unexpected emotions that surged through her was so powerful that her limbs felt weak. Raising her head, she saw a spark leap into his eyes, as if the contact generated the same sensations in him.

''Ex-excuse me,'' she murmured, extricating herself from his involuntary embrace with as much poise as she could muster. She turned away from him and continued in the direction they'd been heading, this time paying special attention to where she stepped. She didn't want to slip and end up in his arms again. She could almost feel his gaze boring into her back, and once, when she glanced behind her, she thought she caught a glimpse of an amused smile.

As they made their way along the bank, she carefully scrutinized the stream bed for any indication that its direction had been tampered with. The water appeared to be flowing along in a perfectly normal manner, however, as if it had been following this same course for hundreds of years.

So intent was Serena on her inspection that she didn't notice the fence until she was almost upon it. She came to a sudden stop. Although the triple strand of barbed wire was the dividing line between Mitch's property and hers, the stream ran on, unhampered.

She steeled herself for his exclamation of triumph as he came up behind her. Instead of the "I told you so" she was expecting, however, he simply looked the situation over, then remarked, "We'd better see what's up ahead." He lifted the top two strands of wire and held the bottom one down with his foot, indicating that she was to go through the opening. Somewhat subdued now that her suspicions hadn't been confirmed, she crossed through, then held the strands apart so he could do the same.

They followed the creek for perhaps another quarter of a mile before locating the source of the trouble. A narrow section had become clogged with a huge pile of brush, deadwood, and other debris. The water, instead of flowing along its usual course, was spreading out and filling the low areas on each side. Several cows were drinking from the newly formed pool, and others, having scented water, were approaching.

Serena turned to face Mitch, her cheeks flaming with embarrassment. "It—it looks as if I owe you an apology. I'm afraid Farley and Homer and I have been so busy that checking the creek is something that was overlooked."

"Could have happened to anyone," Mitch commented with an offhanded shrug. "Nobody can be expected to cover every square inch of a ranch every day. This stuff was probably washed down by last night's rain. Doesn't appear that it's been here long."

Under the circumstances he was being very nice

about the situation. He could afford to be, of course, now that he'd been vindicated. Her New England conscience wouldn't allow her to escape the consequences of her hasty and unfair accusation so easily, however.

"I should have checked before jumping to conclusions," she insisted. "I had no right to accuse you that way."

"No harm done," he replied in an amiable tone. "C'mon, I'll take you back to your truck."

Serena was properly subdued on the trip back. She rode in silence, mentally berating herself for having made such a foolish mistake. It wasn't like her to make snap judgments that way. She might have thought the situation through a little more carefully if only she hadn't been so unbelievably tired. . . .

They came upon several men on horseback who were working a small group of cattle, apparently moving them to another spot. Mitch braked to a halt and stuck his head out the window. "Yo, Sam," he called out.

One of the men wheeled his horse around and rode over to the Blazer.

"Sam, will you take a couple of men and go unclog the creek?" Mitch directed.

"Sure thing, boss."

As Sam started to ride off, Mitch called after him, "It's on the other side of the boundary line, about a quarter of a mile into Double C land."

If Sam was surprised at this request, he gave no indication. "Consider it done," he replied, touching the brim of his hat in a gesture of compliance.

"That wasn't necessary," Serena protested as they

drove on. ''I was going to drive out and take care of it as soon as I got back to the ranch and got some equipment.''

''Until that creek is running free again, your cattle will be coming down close to the boundary line for water,'' Mitch pointed out. ''If they all get to milling around in that one area, the fence is going to get knocked down, and they'll end up on my land. Then we'll have the extra work of getting them separated from my herd and rounded up.''

''Oh,'' she said in a small voice. She'd been naive in thinking he was just being helpful. He was concerned about his own interests, of course.

A few minutes later they pulled up behind Serena's pickup truck. *Well, this is it,* she thought. She'd made a complete idiot of herself. All she wanted to do now was offer Mitch the apology she owed him and then make a quick exit, before she did anything to embarrass herself further.

But before she could slip out, Mitch reached over to catch her hand in his. Sensing his intention, she tried to pull away, but she wasn't quick enough. She couldn't suppress a quick intake of breath as his fingers made contact.

''Look, Serena—'' Mitch began, but his words broke off as he noticed her almost imperceptible frown of pain. He glanced at her questioningly; then a look of understanding came into his eyes. Gently he pulled her hand toward himself and turned it over. She tried to close her fingers, but he drew them open, as carefully as if he were unfolding the delicate petals of a flower.

His expression was sympathetic as he inspected the angry-looking blisters on the soft skin of her palm. However, when he commented, "You'd better get into the habit of wearing gloves," his tone was so matter-of-fact that he might as well have been advising her on doctoring a sick horse.

"They'll heal," she replied, jerking her hand away from him. The last thing she wanted was to have him feeling sorry for her.

But he wasn't finished with his scrutiny. He reached up and tilted her hat back on her head so he could examine the scratch above her eyebrow. "You're gonna kill yourself trying to prove a point," he remarked, a trace of humor in his voice.

Beneath his teasing manner was a serious undertone, however, as if he were genuinely concerned for her well-being. He leaned forward a little to take a closer look at the scratch. Gently he traced one finger along it in a gesture so infinitely tender that sudden tears sprang to her eyes.

Instinct told her that it was time to make her exit, but she couldn't seem to make her muscles and nerves do her bidding. She felt mesmerized by his nearness. . . .

Then his lips were brushing hers, in a kiss that sent her emotions reeling. A sweetness like warm honey spread through her, and her limbs felt weak. As if Mitch sensed her response, the pressure of his lips increased.

When at last they broke apart, she had to lean her

head against the back of the seat to pull her scattered thoughts together.

"Serena?"

"Yes," she answered a little breathlessly, still lost in the wonder of his kiss.

But instead of the tender words she expected to hear, he said, "Serena, why don't you give up this foolish idea of trying to be a rancher? You're too soft for this kind of life. Go back East where you belong before you really get hurt."

She came crashing down from her rosy cloud with a thud. So that was the reason for his sympathy and his tenderness—and for his kiss. He'd even made it sound as if he were genuinely concerned for her well-being.

"I don't need you to tell me how to run my life," she snapped. "Just mind your own business."

Her sudden anger now making her oblivious to the blisters on her hands, she yanked the door open. Mitch called after her, but she didn't look back as she rushed to the pickup truck.

On the drive home she had to admit she wasn't sure who she was more angry with—Mitch for trying to manipulate her, or herself for almost falling for his tactics. Did he think she was so spineless that all he had to do was soften her with a kiss and she would do whatever he suggested? She burned with humiliation at the realization that that must have been exactly the impression she'd given.

*Too soft,* was she? She'd show *him!*

## *Chapter Nine*

Serena had awakened early, even before her alarm went off. Already a crackle of excitement could be felt in the air. She was dressed, breakfasted, and ready to go long before a cloud of dust signaled the approach of a caravan of pickups and other vehicles pulling horse trailers.

Farley had already explained to her that small spreads like the Double C had to depend on the help of neighboring ranchers during roundup and branding. In the next few weeks, when it was time for their neighbors to round up and brand their own cattle, she, Farley, and Homer would return the favor. It seemed a sensible arrangement, one that enabled the small ranches to stay in business.

As the procession made its way to the area behind the barn, Serena realized that she had been subconsciously watching for a sight of the blue Blazer. *Don't be silly*, she chided herself. Mitch wouldn't have to become involved in this reciprocal agreement. He already had a full-time crew and could afford to hire any extra help he needed. Not that it made any difference to her, anyway. They'd manage just fine without his help.

But she had no sooner convinced herself that Mitch's participation—or lack of it—mattered not one whit to her, when she spotted his Blazer just pulling in. What was he doing here? she wondered. The others involved in the roundup had come because they knew their help would be reciprocated, but Mitch didn't have to depend on the other ranchers to get his cattle rounded up and branded. Had he come just to spy on her progress or to gloat over her puny efforts to make a go of ranching?

"Mitch usually comes along and lends a hand just to be neighborly," Farley commented, as though reading her thoughts. "He don't expect to be repaid. He just likes to be in on the action. Folks around here consider a roundup almost a social event. It's a chance to get together with the neighbors and find out what everyone's been up to."

Serena had mixed emotions about his presence. Although there was no doubt that every available pair of hands was needed and welcome, she didn't like the idea of being obligated to him. Besides, she was still embarrassed over their last encounter. She cringed every time she recalled how she'd gone storming over to his ranch with her unfounded accusations. She wasn't quite ready to face him again. She reminded herself, however, that with all this open space she should be able to avoid him for one day.

The sun was just making its appearance over the low mountains to the east when the group of riders headed out across the range. They were anxious to complete the first stage of the day's operation—driving the cattle to the branding corral—while the weather was still cool.

Serena was mounted on a rawboned buckskin gelding called Rowdy. Although she would rather have been on Penny, she knew that if she intended to pull her weight today, she needed to ride one of the horses that was accustomed to working cattle. These animals seemed to know instinctively how to cut one cow from a herd or to flush it from a hiding spot and keep it heading in the right direction. They moved with catlike agility, sensing a headstrong cow's intentions of going its own way and blocking its efforts to do so. Serena had been practicing for several weeks, getting the feel of shifting her weight to compensate for the horse's sudden zigzag movements.

By the time they were out of sight of the ranch and getting into the higher country, the riders began to fan out. They knew their business, and it wasn't long before they had the first group of cattle heading toward the branding corral. At the same time more cattle were being herded from other directions, until eventually all these groups came together into one milling, bawling mass. The riders moved along slowly, being careful not to hurry them.

The cattle that were already in bunches were fairly easy to herd, but others had to be hunted out and then coaxed from their hiding spots. Farley pointed off in the direction of a rocky hillside and suggested Serena start looking for strays up there. At first she was a little apprehensive. She'd never done anything like this before. What if she couldn't find any cows? Or if she did, what if they wouldn't go in the direction she wanted them to? She had visions of the stolid beasts simply standing and staring at her, implacable and unyielding.

But then she discovered, with relief, that Rowdy knew exactly what was expected of him. Despite his unimpressive appearance, her admiration for the rangy, long-legged animal grew as he demonstrated his skill at finding strays and flushing them out.

"Sorry I didn't have much faith in you, boy," she murmured, first making sure that nobody was around to hear her talking to a horse. "You know I'm counting on you to keep me from looking like too much of a tenderfoot."

Serena and Rowdy chased cows up and down hills, out of rocky gullies, through thick brush. The creatures seemed to have a talent for finding out-of-the-way places to hide, where it was almost impossible to drive them out.

For a while Serena was enjoying the challenge. Each time she located a cow that preferred to stay hidden, she felt a sense of accomplishment. After several hours, however, her enthusiasm began to wane. The elusive animals seemed to be getting more creative in finding hiding places and more resistant to her attempts to flush them out. Eventually she concluded that cattle had to be the most stubborn creatures alive. And it didn't help that she could feel the sweat running down her back in little rivulets, that her throat was so dry and parched she could barely swallow, and that her legs felt as if they were permanently molded around her horse.

But as tired as she was, she couldn't quit—not after all those other people had turned out to help with the roundup. Besides, she wasn't going to let a bunch of cows get the best of her. With grim determination she made her way around a huge, jutting boulder, in pursuit of a particularly strong-willed beast.

Suddenly she came upon Mitch bearing down on the animal from the other side. With a panicky expression, the cow made a sudden turn and attempted to run in the opposite direction. At a barely perceptible signal from Mitch, his horse wheeled around to head off its escape. It looked around wildly and tried to squeeze past Serena. Almost instinctively she nudged Rowdy into a sidestep that blocked its way.

Mitch broke into a grin as he removed one hand from the reins long enough to bring his thumb and forefinger together in a gesture that indicated his approval of her quick thinking.

The next move was Mitch's, and he patiently worked the animal until it was past the boulder. Then Serena took over, keeping it from breaking away. Thus, they made their way down the slope with the cow between them, silently communicating to each other across the twenty or so feet that separated them.

By the time they reached a small bunch of cattle that was being driven toward the corral, the fight had gone out of the stray, and it seemed resigned to its fate. Serena watched with satisfaction as it joined the rest of the herd.

"We make a pretty good team," Mitch called to her with a jaunty wave as he wheeled his horse around and rode off.

Serena had a feeling of accomplishment. The brief episode had restored her good spirits, and she resumed her appointed task with a new vigor.

By noontime most of the herd had been driven down. Then the fast, hot, dusty job of branding the calves began. Taking a much-needed break, Serena perched on a fence rail and watched the proceedings with interest. At first everything merged together into a confused impression of frightened, bawling calves, white, billowing smoke mixed with clouds of dust, and the pungent smell of burned hair.

Eventually the procedure began to sort itself out. She was able to see that everything was done according to a set pattern, with hardly a wasted movement. Once the calf was roped, two husky lads went into action, wrestling it to the ground. She could see they were teenagers, football players by the look of them, and they seemed to be enjoying the opportunity to demonstrate their skill and strength.

With quick, well-coordinated motions, they soon had the calf in position for branding. One braced his foot against the animal's hindquarters while stretching its top hind leg taut. The other boy gripped the front leg so it couldn't get up.

As soon as it was in position, a little flurry of activity took place as it was branded, vaccinated, dehorned, and the male calves castrated, all in a matter of minutes.

The first few times Serena witnessed this procedure,

she could barely restrain herself from jumping down from the fence and shouting, *Stop, you're killing my calves!* She was convinced that no animal could survive such brutal treatment. She relaxed somewhat when she saw how briskly the calves scampered back to their mothers as soon as they were released. She still couldn't help wincing, however, each time the branding iron came down on an animal's hindquarters.

"It's not as bad as it looks," a voice next to her said. "The calves are almost as upset about being separated from their mothers as they are over what's being done to them."

Serena turned her head in surprise. She'd been so involved in what was going on that she hadn't noticed Mitch next to her, leaning his arms over the top rail of the fence. Now she was embarrassed that he'd seen her distress. If she expected him to take her efforts at ranching seriously, she couldn't go around acting as if the cattle were *pets*.

But he seemed to understand her feelings. "Nobody likes to inflict pain on them, but all these procedures are necessary," he explained. "I won't try to tell you it doesn't hurt them some, but the experienced ranch hands know how to make it as quick and painless as possible."

She appreciated his efforts to make her feel better. Why was it, she wondered, that every time she made up her mind that he was bullheaded, arrogant, and egotistical, he threw her off balance by demonstrating a tender, caring side of his personality?

Inexplicably, she felt a wetness prickling the backs

of her eyelids. She wasn't sure if it was caused by Mitch's unexpected sympathy, her own concern for the poor, frightened calves, or merely her exhaustion. If the tears were allowed to run down her cheeks unhampered, they would make streaks in the layer of dust that covered her face. Yet she didn't dare call attention to them by reaching up to wipe them away. The last thing she wanted to do in front of Mitch was to display weakness by crying. Keeping her face averted, she climbed down from the fence and walked away.

While the calf branding continued, Serena kept busy with a variety of odd jobs. While she worked, she kept note of where Mitch was and what he was doing, so she could stay as far away from him as possible. That seemed the sensible thing to do, since almost every encounter with him stirred up her emotions in one way or another. Right now she was feeling puzzled and confused by his unanticipated compassion. Something about the way he had sensed her distress and had taken the time to reassure her had left her with a warm, almost melting feeling.

And with this warmth came the memory of being in his arms. Even now she could recall the touch, the taste, the feel of his lips on hers. . . .

But she had to stop this right now. There was important work to be done, and she couldn't waste time daydreaming just because Mitch had once responded to what she now knew had been nothing but a physical attraction on his part. Common sense told her the wisest thing she could do would be to put him out of her mind completely.

Yet she knew she could no more do that than she could stop breathing. For in the remote, secret reaches of her heart, she had admitted she was hopelessly, irrevocably in love with Mitch Tanner. And since she had little reason to believe that love would ever be reciprocated, her only other option was to make sure he never discovered the depths of her feelings for him. She sighed heavily. It would be a relief when the day's activities were over; trying to avoid Mitch was a strain.

By now the last of the new calves had been branded, and the crew had started in on the two-year-old heifers. Since these animals were too big for even the most determined cowhand to wrestle down, the squeeze chute was put to use. As each heifer was prodded through, it was simultaneously vaccinated and given a brand on the shoulder that denoted the year it was born.

After this was finished, the neighbors would go home. Some of them would return the next day, however, to help with the few remaining jobs, such as driving the breeding bulls to the summer pasture. Serena had mixed emotions about whether she hoped Mitch would show up.

"Serena, you busy right now?" Farley's voice cut into her thoughts.

"No, I was just about to come looking for you to see what else needs to be done."

"Looks like we missed a few heifers. A couple of them were spotted up on the east ridge. You want to ride up and see if you can find 'em?"

"Sure, I'll be glad to." By now it was late in the afternoon, and she was tired. Still, she was glad to have a good reason to leave the site, so she wouldn't have to continually be on guard against running into Mitch.

Although she headed Rowdy off in the direction Farley had indicated, she found no sign of the missing heifers. It was possible that they had moved on by now or that some of the other riders had located them and driven them in. She wasn't ready to give up searching for them yet, however. Each of these animals represented funds to pay for needed repairs around the ranch, buy feed and equipment, and make mortgage payments.

The late-afternoon sun was spreading grotesque shadows across the rough, uneven terrain by the time she finally located three heifers hiding in a gully with steep, rocky walls on three sides. At first they resisted her efforts to drive them out, crowding closer together at the far end of the long, narrow space. Then, as she worked her way closer to them, they were suddenly galvanized into action. In a panic they thudded past her and squeezed through the small opening.

Serena wheeled Rowdy around, but by the time horse and rider were back out in the open, the trio was just disappearing into a thick stand of trees. Muttering to herself in exasperation, she nudged Rowdy into a trot.

She was almost tempted to turn back and forget these last three cows, but she was reluctant to give up without having accomplished her mission, especially if Mitch would be there to see her return in defeat. She felt her honor and pride were at stake. She headed Rowdy in the direction the animals had gone and nudged him into a trot.

For perhaps an hour she trailed the elusive heifers, who managed to stay just ahead of her. So intent was she on her pursuit that she barely noticed the sky fading from blue to gray or the way the contours of the landscape were becoming blurred and indistinct.

"Just a little while longer," she murmured to Rowdy. By now she was incredibly weary. She was beginning to feel as if her entire life had been spent in the saddle, her hands gripping the reins. "If we don't find them soon, we'll head back," she promised.

*Might as well give it up,* she finally decided. Before long it would be dark, and she wouldn't be able to see the heifers even if she did catch up with them. Reluctantly she reined Rowdy around, feeling as if she'd failed.

A shiver of apprehension went through her as she scanned the area spread before her for familiar landmarks. She'd taken so many twists and turns in her pursuit of the cows that she had no idea which direction she'd come from.

With a shrug Serena decided this was as good a time as any to find out if it was true that horses could always find their way back to the barn. "I guess it's up to you," she said, giving the animal its head.

Although she told herself that there was nothing to worry about, that Rowdy would get them both home, she couldn't help tensing up with each shift of direction or position. She felt utterly helpless as the horse picked his way across the uneven ground. It was becoming more and more difficult to see, and she had only his surefootedness and his homing instinct to depend on.

When she sensed that they were starting to descend a steep slope, she gave up any pretense of being in charge and clung to the saddle horn tightly. She devoutly hoped that horses could see in the dark.

She could hear the loose gravel under Rowdy's hooves, and occasionally there was a clatter as a rock was displaced and went rolling down the hill. From the way the noise went on and on, this must be an awfully steep grade.

After what seemed an eternity, they came to a spot where the incline leveled off slightly. Serena began to breathe a little easier. She released her grip and allowed her body to relax. "You're doing fine," she whispered to the horse, more for her own benefit and reassurance than for his. Although she knew he couldn't understand her words, the sound of a voice, even her own, was comforting.

It happened so suddenly she had no time to react. Rowdy put his foot down in a low spot, and one leg started to buckle. Although he righted himself almost immediately, that split second was all it took. She made a frantic grab for his mane, the saddle horn, *anything* to regain her balance, but it was too late. She felt herself slipping from the saddle, and there was nothing she could do to stop her fall.

Serena fought her way out of a deep, heavy darkness, blacker than anything she'd ever experienced. She was vaguely aware of Rowdy standing over her, nickering softly.

Her head ached abominably. When she tried to push herself to a sitting position, the pain exploded into a million sharp pieces that permeated every part of her. She couldn't hold back a low moan. Then she was slipping off into oblivion again.

The next time she awoke, the pain had subsided to a dull throb. She opened her eyes and gazed about her, without moving. All she could see were the stars overhead, fuzzy and unfocused. Gradually they sharpened into frosty pinpoints of light on a velvet background. She wondered how long she'd been unconscious. A few minutes? Several hours? From the sore, cramped condition of her muscles, it must have been quite a while.

She lay still, assessing her predicament. Here she was, lost in the middle of who-knew-where. She suppressed a slightly hysterical giggle as the phrase *This is another fine mess you've gotten us into* popped into her mind. She decided that was a good sign. She couldn't be too badly off if she could still laugh.

Lying here wasn't going to accomplish anything, she told herself. Besides, a sharp stone was digging into her ribs. As she got up slowly, experimentally, the world tilted and spun at a crazy angle before righting itself.

She wondered what had become of Rowdy. Most likely he had followed his natural instinct and returned to the ranch. A search for her would be started, of course, as soon as he showed up without her. There was a lot of ground to cover, however, and it might be a long time before she was found. She decided she'd be better off to start walking. By now her eyes were beginning to adjust to the darkness, and she glanced around for any landmark that would show her which direction to take. She saw nothing but rocks, trees, and shrubs, all looking eerie and mysterious in the moonlight.

*Downhill, of course,* her common sense told her. And maybe by the time she reached level ground, she'd be able to get her bearings.

Slowly, cautiously, she began to make her way down the rocky incline, wincing with every step. She put each foot down carefully, making sure it was on solid ground before placing her weight on it. If she stepped in a hole or on some loose rock, she could go tumbling down the hill. She was in a serious enough position as it was, without taking the chance of breaking a bone or two.

When she reached a spot that was relatively flat, she stopped to rest, easing herself down to a reclining position and pillowing her head on her arms. Just the short distance she'd come had taken its toll on her flagging strength. Maybe she'd be better off to just stay here until someone found her. She might even try to sleep a little. It would feel so good to just close her eyes. . . .

But she remembered hearing that a person with a head injury shouldn't be allowed to go to sleep. She sat up so suddenly that the pounding in her head, which had begun to subside, started in again with a vengeance. Well, even if she couldn't sleep, she could at least rest here for a while. She was so incredibly weary.

A faint rustling off to one side jolted her out of her lethargy. She sat stock still, every muscle of her body tense, as she strained to make out the source of the noise. It was probably nothing but a gopher or some other small furry creature, she told herself. But another possibility, one that she'd tried to ignore, pushed its way into her mind. What if it was a rattlesnake? She could picture it slithering along the rough, uneven ground, dislodging an occasional twig or loose stone.

At that moment the sound came again, closer than before—or so it seemed. She jumped up, her fright making her temporarily oblivious to the pain in her head. Her heart was thudding, and her breath came in little gasps as she scrambled down the hill and away from whatever was making that noise.

In her haste she lost her footing and slid several feet. By the time she was able to slow her descent, she was sore and bruised where the jagged rocks had dug into her soft flesh.

Eventually she came to level ground, and her way became easier. By now the throbbing in her head was worse. And she was so cold—the chilly dampness sent its icy fingers into her very bones. As she walked she rubbed her upper arms, trying to massage some warmth into them.

Several times she could have sworn she detected something moving in the darkness. Although she tried to convince herself the shadows she was seeing were caused by clouds moving across the moon's face, certain questions kept popping into her mind—such as, Why was the nearby community called *Cougar* Bluff? Why not something like *Raccoon* Bluff or *Gopher* Bluff? Resolutely, she put the question out of her thoughts. There were certain aspects of her situation she preferred not to dwell on.

She lost track of time as she stumbled along, with barely enough strength to put one foot in front of the other. It seemed she had been walking forever. She longed to stop and rest, but she knew that if she did, she'd fall asleep. Even if her head injury might not be serious enough to warrant staying awake, she didn't want to be asleep if searchers came looking for her. She envisioned them passing right by, unable to see her as she lay hidden behind some brush or a boulder.

In the distance she could hear the occasional howl of coyotes, their high-pitched wails floating eerily through the night air. And once she saw an owl silently gliding by, its wings outstretched, silhouetted against the moonlit sky. She watched as it descended, talons outstretched, toward a jumble of rocks and brush several yards away.

Just as it merged into the shadows and became invisible, a faint scuffling noise broke the stillness. It was accompanied by a brief, high-pitched yelp—almost like a scream. She shuddered when it was cut off abruptly.

By the time the first faint streaks of light began to show, she was reaching the limits of her strength and endurance. Although the jagged peaks to the east were gilded by delicate fingers of pink and gold, the splendor of the sunrise was lost on her. The pain in her head was increasing, and she was so cold that she couldn't remember ever having been warm.

Even worse than the ache and the numbing cold was her unbelievable weariness. If she allowed herself to sleep, she might never wake up. Yet if she didn't rest soon, she was sure she would collapse. How much longer could she wander around out here? she wondered. The thought of lying down and closing her eyes was so tempting. . . .

But Serena's instinct of self-preservation was strong. She forced herself to continue her plodding way. By now the hills had flattened out. She stumbled across a broad expanse of open plain that stretched to a horizon of low purple mountains.

When she spotted the silver speck moving slowly toward her, she hardly dared hope what she saw was real. It could be a figment of her imagination, something she had conjured up in her desperation. She was afraid to even blink. If she took her eyes away from the sight for a second, it might be gone when she looked back. Even the low drone that emanated from it didn't seem real. She wondered if the sound was inside her head, a side effect of her head injury.

As the airplane banked slowly, a ray of the early-morning sun caught its window glass, or maybe a bit of metal. For a brief moment a shaft of pure gold shot out from it, so brilliant it hurt her eyes.

She watched with growing anticipation as the small craft made lazy circles overhead, moving closer to her each time. Although she couldn't make out the airplane's markings, some inner sense told her that it was Mitch's Cherokee and that he was at the controls. It was obvious that he was making a methodical search.

What if he failed to spot her? The terrain around her was dotted with rocks and brush, and she could easily be overlooked. Each time the airplane's circle took it in the opposite direction, her heart jumped into her throat as she wondered if he had given up looking here and was moving on to another area.

Finally she could stand it no longer. With trembling fingers she untied the bandanna around her neck. Waving it above her head like a flag, she went running out across the plain.

When the plane's wings dipped, she knew that everything was going to be all right. Mitch was signaling to her that he'd spotted her. The tears that had never been far from the surface during the long, terrifying night now flowed down her cheeks unhampered as she watched Mitch make one more circle, picking out a suitable landing spot.

He was out of the plane and running toward her almost before the wheels had stopped rolling. Serena's last reserves of strength and self-control deserted her as she stumbled into his arms.

Just before blackness descended on her, she caught a glimpse of Mitch's expression. Suffering was etched in the sharp planes and angles of his face, and his eyes revealed a tortured dullness, as if he'd just emerged from some painful ordeal.

And beneath it all was something she couldn't identify. A sort of—tenderness. Then she yielded to the weakness that was taking control of her. As she sagged wearily, she felt his strong arms supporting her.

Although she was beyond rational thought, her instincts told her everything would be all right now. Mitch was here to take care of her. Resting her head against his chest, she could hear his heart beating next to her ear. The sound was soothing, lulling her to sleep. . . .

Her last awareness was of his deep, gentle voice. It seemed to be whispering words of endearment. Had he actually called her *darling,* or had she only imagined it?

# *Chapter Ten*

Serena was suspended in a haze of gray, swirling mist. She made a halfhearted attempt to brush the vaporous tendrils aside, but it seemed to take more strength than she had. It was so much easier to just lie here. She sank back weakly and let the shadows close in around her.

After a while she had a vague sensation of being carried, or transported somehow. She could hear a low murmur of voices around her, but trying to concentrate on what was being said was too much trouble. She did make out something about, "... could have been seriously injured...." She wondered whom they were talking about. Once somebody shone a bright light in her eyes. She wished they would all just go away and leave her alone.

She had been having the most delightful dream, and people kept interrupting. In this dream Mitch was holding her as if she were something fragile and precious, and she felt utterly safe and protected in his arms. As she rested her head against his chest, drawing strength from him, he was telling her how much he loved her and how worried he'd been about her. And then he brushed a gentle kiss across her forehead. . . .

Eventually consciousness returned, and with it rational thought.

Serena lay in the big, comfortable bed in the guest room at the Diamond T, clad in a man's white shirt several sizes too large for her.

Although the events of the past few hours were still scrambled together in a confused jumble, she was able to sort them out into some kind of order. She had only a hazy memory of what had taken place immediately after she'd collapsed into Mitch's arms, but she vaguely recalled being met by a small crowd when the airplane landed and Mitch telling them, "We'll take her to my place—it's closer."

Somehow—in the Blazer, she supposed—she was transported to Mitch's house, where Cloris, his housekeeper, produced one of his shirts to serve as a nightgown and tenderly tucked her into bed. The doctor arrived shortly thereafter. Her scratches and bruises were treated, and the lump on her head was examined and pronounced, "Not serious."

"What she needs more than anything is a good long rest," the doctor said. "She's young and strong and will be fine."

Then everyone had tiptoed out and left her to get some much-needed sleep.

Serena was debating whether to try getting up, when her thoughts were interrupted by a light tap at the door, accompanied by a voice calling softly, ''Are you awake?''

''Yes, come in,'' she replied.

The door opened, and Cloris entered, carrying a tray. ''I didn't want to disturb you if you were still asleep,'' she said, ''but I thought you might be ready for something to eat.'' She put the tray on a table next to the bed and scrutinized Serena. ''You have to keep your strength up, you know. You've been through a trying experience.'' Fussing like a mother hen, she rearranged Serena's pillows and helped her to a sitting position. When she was satisfied that her patient was comfortable, she put the tray on her lap.

While Serena ate, Cloris kept up a steady flow of talk. ''Mitch certainly was worried about you. I've looked after him since he was a boy, and I don't recall ever seeing him so upset. He took his plane out and hunted for you until it was so dark, it was dangerous to be flying. Of course, there were others out looking too. . . .''

From Cloris's conversation Serena gathered that a search had been organized as soon as her horse had come back, riderless and limping slightly. The search party had started with those who had taken part in the roundup but had quickly expanded as the word spread. Besides the riders, those with four-wheel-drive vehicles had also been out scouring the countryside. The search was finally called off because of darkness, but Mitch had stubbornly refused to come in until the last possible minute.

''He hardly slept at all last night,'' Cloris went on.

"I could hear him pacing in the middle of the night. Then he was out again this morning almost before daylight."

Serena's first reaction was a little thrill of pleased surprise at learning that Mitch had gone to so much trouble to look for her. She reminded herself, however, that it was no more than he'd have done for anyone who was lost out on the range.

When she finished eating, Cloris whisked the tray away and regarded her approvingly. "You're looking better already. Getting a little color back in your cheeks. There's nothing like a good meal to cure whatever ails a person, I always say."

Serena couldn't help smiling at Cloris's homespun wisdom. Still, there must be some truth to it. She *was* feeling stronger. Besides, it was time she was up and around. She needed to get dressed and then arrange for someone to come and get her. "I think I'd like to get up now," she said.

"I washed your things while you were asleep." Cloris indicated the pile of neatly folded clothing on a chair. "I thought you'd like some fresh clothes to put on. Will you be able to manage by yourself?"

"I'm sure I will." She didn't want to cause any more trouble to anyone than she already had.

"You'll find towels and whatever else you need in there," Cloris said, nodding toward the bathroom that adjoined the guest room. "I always keep a few new combs and toothbrushes in the drawer."

When Cloris had left the room, Serena got out of bed cautiously. Her muscles were stiff and sore, and her head still had a tendency to throb if she made any sudden motions. She concentrated on keeping her movements slow and deliberate.

After she was showered and dressed, she went in search of a telephone. Nobody seemed to be around as she descended the stairs. Cloris was nowhere in sight, and she didn't expect to see Mitch. Most likely he was out making up for the time he'd lost while helping with the Double C roundup and then searching for her.

She peeked into several rooms in the sprawling house, feeling like an intruder. She wasn't accustomed to poking about in other people's homes when the occupants weren't around. Although she'd been here once before, it had only been for a few moments, and she'd been too upset at the time to pay attention to the layout of the big, rambling structure.

She spotted a wide doorway that looked as if it might lead to the main part of the house. Surely she'd find a telephone in there. As she started to enter the room, a tall figure coming through the door from the opposite direction suddenly loomed up in front of her. Taken by surprise, she was unable to stop, and a collision was unavoidable. She ran smack into Mitch with such force that she almost lost her balance.

He instinctively reached out to steady her, and Serena inhaled sharply at the contact. Even through the thin material of her shirt, his touch aroused a tingling sensation, as if currents of electricity were flowing through her. She told herself this unexpected reaction was due to her weakened condition. And of course she was still feeling the effects of that dream she'd had while she was in a semiconscious state.

His brow furrowed in concern. "Hey, did I hurt you?"

Serena realized, with relief, that he was attributing her startled gasp to their sudden collision.

"I—I'm fine," she stammered, although that wasn't altogether true. She seemed to be having a little trouble catching her breath, and her heart had begun to pound at an alarming rate. She wondered if she might be having a relapse. Maybe she shouldn't have gotten up so soon. "I—ah—was just going to find a telephone and call the Double C to have someone come and get me."

"That won't be necessary. I'll drive you home."

She wasn't sure that was such a good idea. Until she recovered from the impact of that startlingly vivid dream, it might not be wise to be alone with him. "I don't want to keep you from your work. Just tell me where the phone is, and I'll call Farley."

"I said I'll take you." His tone was quietly authoritative.

Goodness, was he in that big a hurry to get her out of his house? she wondered.

"Farley and Homer are still out moving those bulls to the summer pasture," he explained.

"Oh. Well, in that case. . . ." Her words trailed off as she became aware that he was standing awfully close, so close that she could see the flecks of gold that highlighted his dark eyes. So close she could reach up and trace the outline of his lips with her finger. . . .

*Stop that,* she told herself firmly. If he'd quit looking at her that way, maybe she could collect her wits. But his nearness made it difficult to think rationally.

He had apparently forgotten that his hands were still on her shoulders. With what little self-possession Serena had left, she backed away, carefully extricating herself.

The silence was starting to become uncomfortable. "I—I guess I have quite a lot to thank you for," she said. "I understand you were the one who found me and brought me back."

His features darkened into a frown, as if he'd just remembered the reason she was here in the first place. "Do you realize how foolish you were to go riding off where you didn't know the territory?" His tone was stern.

At once the spell was broken. "I didn't get lost on purpose," Serena shot back.

"That's not the point. You should have been more careful. When I think of all the things that could have happened to you while you were wandering around out there in the dark— Wild animals. You could have fallen over a cliff. . . ."

A surge of anger coursed through Serena. What right did he have to reprimand her as if she were a child who had misbehaved? Although she was aware that she owed him a great deal for finding her, she wasn't in any mood to be scolded. Now that she'd been up for a while, her legs were weak and shaky, and her head was starting to throb again.

"I'm sorry to have been such a bother to you." Her

attempt at haughtiness failed miserably, and she had to struggle just to keep her voice from trembling. "I'll have to accept your offer of a ride because it seems it's the only way I can get home, but after that I won't trouble you again."

"That's fine with me. If you want to be so independent, then the next time you get lost, you can darned well *stay* lost."

"All right, I will!" Although Serena realized how childish that sounded, she couldn't resist saying it. What was it about this man that always brought out the worst in her? "What business is it of yours, anyway?" she demanded.

He glared at her, his face like a thundercloud. "It just happens that I don't like to see someone I care about in danger. I'm funny that way."

"And I don't like being lectured by someone *I* care about—" She broke off in midsentence as it occurred to her what an abrupt change in direction this argument was taking. As they stood facing each other, Serena felt her anger draining away, to be replaced by confusion and some other emotion she couldn't quite identify.

"Oh, there you are." The tense moment was broken by Cloris's appearance. "Did you find the telephone? It's over there in the corner."

"Serena won't be needing the phone. I'll drive her home." Mitch's voice and manner were restrained.

Cloris started to say something else, then seemed to catch herself as she glanced from Mitch to Serena. It was obvious that *something* was in the air. She excused herself with, "I—ah—think I hear the stove timer." Neither party seemed to notice as she backed out of the room and made a hasty exit.

"If you're ready, we can be going now," Mitch said, as if nothing unusual had occurred between them.

"Yes, of course," Serena replied in the same politely impersonal tone Mitch had used.

They maintained this courteously reserved attitude all the way back to the Double C, speaking very little and only about the most general of subjects. Serena had a sinking feeling she had said too much already. What had Mitch's exact words been? ". . . someone I care about. . . ." and her response had been automatic.

*Someone I care about* was such an ambiguous phrase. For her part, what she felt for Mitch went far beyond just "caring" for him. She'd already admitted to herself that she was deeply in love with him.

In Mitch's case the phrase could mean something entirely different. *Someone I care about* didn't necessarily indicate any romantic feelings. It could—and most likely did—refer to any acquaintance for whom he felt at least a passing concern. She *was* the daughter of an old friend of his, so naturally he wouldn't want any harm to come to her, even if he did consider her a nuisance. He would likely be at least as worried if—say—Cloris or one of the ranch hands had been in danger.

But what if he *had* been echoing what was in his heart—that he was as attracted to her as she was to him? What if, in the heat of the argument, he'd accidentally revealed his true feelings, just as her own had inadvertently slipped out?

Even if that were the case, where did they go from here? she wondered. The next move, if there was to be one, had to come from him.

Serena had intended to slip out of the Blazer as soon as it came to a stop, tossing a brief "Thank you" over her shoulder. Mitch made it clear, however, that he wouldn't consider his duty finished until he had seen her safely to her door.

"I can manage . . ." she began, but her voice trailed off after a quick glance at his determined features. As he escorted her across the lawn, she was disturbingly aware of his touch, firm but infinitely gentle, under her arm. She wondered if he had any idea of the effect that contact had on her.

His parting remark, after he had ushered her into the house and she'd convinced him that she would be all right by herself, was, "I'll be over to see you later. We have unfinished business to discuss—when we're both calmer." With that he turned and strode away, leaving her to stare after him in astonishment.

As she watched him drive off, she wondered what he'd meant by that last remark. Did "later" mean tomorrow or next week? Or perhaps this evening? And what did he want to see her about when they couldn't seem to find anything to say to each other on the ride home?

Most likely he was just giving her a chance to regain her strength before he redoubled his efforts to convince her to sell the Double C to him. Of course—that would be the "unfinished business" he'd referred to. He probably intended to use her getting lost as further proof of how unsuited she was to ranch life.

As Serena went about the evening chores, she thought over the events of the day. Farley had been almost touchingly relieved at her safe return, and even the taciturn Homer had admitted that he'd "shore been worried" about her. Neither had wanted to allow her to take over her share of the chores just yet, but she'd refused to be treated as an invalid.

The telephone had rung several times since her return, with neighbors calling to inquire after her well-being. Many of them had stories to relate about knowing someone who had had a similar experience. This went a long way toward dispelling the embarrassment she was feeling at having caused so many people to take time away from their busy schedules to search for her.

After the chores were finished, she lingered in the barn, watching Lucky in the box stall with his mother. The colt was growing rapidly and showed every indication of developing into an outstanding example of his breed. She felt a sense of satisfaction as she rested her arms on the railing of the stall and admired his clean, graceful lines.

Lucky's ears pricked up alertly as someone entered the barn. Serena glanced up, expecting Farley or Homer, and was surprised to see Mitch approaching.

He had changed his clothes since he'd dropped her off this afternoon. Although they were similar to his usual garb of jeans and casual shirt, these were a little nicer than the ones he wore to work around the ranch. Even his boots were free of the layer of dust that covered them most of the time. When he came near, he exuded a tangy male scent, as if he had just showered and shaved.

Besides his attire, something else was different about him. His usual air of self-assurance seemed to have been replaced by a sort of hesitancy that was quite out of character for him. What was he up to now? she wondered. She watched warily as he nodded a greeting to her and took up a position similar to hers, leaning on the rail to watch Lucky.

"We did a good job of bringing him into the world, didn't we?" he commented, his glance indicating the colt.

That seemed a safe-enough topic. "Yes, we did," she agreed.

For several moments there were no sounds except the rustling of straw as the animals moved around in their stalls. As the silence began to stretch, Mitch ventured, "We'd probably make a good team in a lot of other ways."

Serena kept her eyes straight ahead, on the mare and colt. She was aware that he was doing the same. What was he working up to? She recalled the "unfinished business" he'd mentioned. Maybe he was going to suggest she sell him an interest in the Double C so that he could have a say in its operation and she wouldn't have to give it up completely. That might be an acceptable compromise, except for one thing—she doubted she'd be able to work closely with him without giving away her feelings.

"What did you have in mind?" she asked, still not looking his way. "Some kind of partnership?"

"Not exactly. The arrangement I was thinking of was more—personal."

*Personal?* She turned her head in his direction. Her breath caught in her throat as she found herself looking directly into his eyes.

"That remark I made this afternoon, about not wanting to see people I care about in danger—"

Time stood still as she waited for him to go on.

"I hadn't planned to blurt it out that way. I meant to use a little more finesse to let you know I love you."

Serena's world spun and tilted crazily. "Why—why didn't you tell me sooner?" she asked when she finally found her voice.

His grave expression was replaced by a grin so engaging that it went straight to her heart and set it singing. "I tried to tell you this morning, but you wouldn't stay awake long enough. It's hard to tell a woman you love her when she keeps falling asleep."

Then he turned serious again. "I'd been trying to convince myself for a long time that there could never be anything between us—that we come from two different worlds. But last night, when your horse came back without you and I didn't know what kind of danger you were in, I finally had to stop denying what I feel. All that time I was out searching for you, I promised myself that once I found you, I wouldn't let another day go by without making sure you knew how much you meant to me. Even though you were barely conscious by the time I carried you to the plane, I hoped at least a little of what I was saying was getting through."

So it *hadn't* been a dream! A burst of pure joy radiated through Serena. "I did hear you. I—I thought I'd dreamed it."

"I really blew it this afternoon, didn't I?" Mitch admitted. "What I really wanted to do was take you in my arms and never let you go, but you looked so—so fragile that I didn't dare touch you. And seeing you that way reminded me of how easily I could have lost you. I guess that's when I just sort of fell apart."

Although a million thoughts tumbled through Serena's mind, she was too overcome with emotion to voice any of them.

It was obvious, from the concern in Mitch's face, that he was misinterpreting her silence. "Is—is there still a chance for us?" he asked, anxiety making his tone harsh and ragged. "Or is it too late? Have I ruined everything with that rotten temper of mine?"

"Yes!" Serena managed to get out. "I mean no," she amended, confused. "No, it isn't too late, and yes, there's a chance for us!"

Then somehow she was in Mitch's arms, laughing and crying at the same time. Although he was kissing her tenderly, his ardor was restrained. Mindful of her bruises, he was as gentle with her as if she were a piece of rare porcelain.

"You don't have to be that careful," Serena whispered. "I won't break."

Mitch drew back to look into her eyes. "All right, you asked for it," he warned, drawing her close. "C'mere, woman." His voice, low and husky, sent tingles of anticipation through her.

This time his kiss was thorough, masterful, and fully satisfying.

"Now then," he said when they finally broke apart, "there are some things we have to get settled." The warmth in his eyes belied his brisk, businesslike tone.

"Whatever you say," she murmured docilely. She gave a little sigh of contentment as she rested her cheek against his chest and gazed up at him.

"Here's the situation. . . ." He paused to brush a fleeting kiss across her forehead. He seemed to lose his train of thought as his eyes met hers.

"Yes?" she prompted.

"What? Oh, where was I?"

"I think you were about to make some masterful, authoritative pronouncement," she reminded him.

"Oh. I remember. I was going to tell you that I know I should take time to court you properly, for a couple of months, at least—dinner and movie dates in Cougar Bluff so folks will know we're 'keeping company,' walks in the moonlight, that sort of thing. I hate to rush you, but I don't think I can wait that long. . . ." Between sentences his lips were tracing enticing patterns from the corners of her mouth to her throat. "We've wasted too much time already. How soon can we be married?" He nuzzled her earlobe as he waited for her reply.

At first her practical side thought of a multitude of

reasons why they should go into this carefully. But then, as Mitch's gentle caresses awakened ripples of longing in her, she threw caution to the winds. "As soon as you like," she murmured.

With a whoop of sheer jubilation, he picked her up and swung her around exuberantly. Then, remembering her weakened condition, he set her down gently. "Well, then, what are we waiting for? I suppose you'll need some kind of wedding dress—although you look fine to me," he said, eyeing her form-fitting jeans and the way the lightweight material of her shirt molded her contours. "We can drive into Cougar Bluff and find you a dress to get married in, and while we're there, we'll get the license and some flowers—am I going too fast for you?"

## *Chapter Eleven*

"Now, you be mighty careful out there," Farley warned as Serena finished saddling and bridling Penny. "Mitch wouldn't take it too well if we let anything happen to you," he drawled.

"Don't worry, I've learned my lesson," she replied with a rueful laugh. What she had learned was that, in spite of its rugged beauty, this country was harsh and unforgiving toward those who failed to give it the proper respect.

After her close call she had vowed she would never get caught that way again. And now that she had given up all thought of returning to Windham, it was especially important that she familiarize herself with every aspect of the region that was to be her permanent home. There were areas of her own ranch she had never seen, mainly because the never-ending round of chores had left her with little time or energy left over for sightseeing.

But now, with her marriage to Mitch less than a week away, Farley and Homer had insisted she take some time off to rest up and get ready for her wedding. When she'd protested that there was too much work to be done, they'd pointed out that once she became Mrs. Mitch Tanner and the two ranches were combined, Mitch's crew of ranch hands would take over some of the Double C chores.

"Now that there won't be just the three of us trying to do it all, there ain't no big rush," Farley had reminded her. "Go on and enjoy yourself."

Serena was looking forward to a relaxing ride on Penny, with nothing more urgent to do than meander and seek out heretofore unexplored corners of the ranch. And even the areas she had already seen, she would now be looking at with new eyes. Until a few days ago she had considered herself to be here temporarily. Even after learning that she no longer had a job or apartment to return to in Windham, she had assumed that eventually she would go back. Now that she knew she was staying here, however, she took a proprietary pride in every tree and shrub, every rock and boulder on the Double C.

"Be seeing you later," she called to Farley as she swung into the saddle and whistled for Max to accompany her.

She gave Penny her head, and the little mare daintily picked her way along the path of the creek, stopping occasionally to munch the lush, sweet grass that grew alongside it. When they neared the fence, Serena nudged her to the right. If they followed the boundary line between her ranch and the Diamond T, there would be little chance of getting lost again.

She gazed in admiration at the rich panorama of mountains and hills, valleys and gorges spread out before her. Everything about her surroundings seemed heightened and enhanced, the sky so intensely blue that the peaks and ridges silhouetted against it stood out in sharp relief. Wide sweeps of open plain gave way to dark-timbered slopes and jagged cliffs sculpted by time and the elements into other-worldly shapes.

And the colors! The gray-green of sagebrush gradually blended with the soft lavender of the low foothills. Brilliant mauves and purples of granite crags contrasted sharply with the icy blue of the mountains in the distance.

It was hard to believe this was the same region that had seemed so terrifying during her all-night ordeal a week ago. That experience was nothing more than a bad dream now. Just as her bruises and scratches were healing, the frightening memories were also fading.

*There's nothing like being in love to put everything in a new light,* Serena thought. She knew her present sense of contentment and well-being was due to loving Mitch and knowing she was loved in return. A delightful shiver ran through her as she relived every moment of that scene in the barn, when Mitch had revealed his feelings for her.

Eventually, of course, they'd emerged from the private little world they'd created long enough to make plans for their future. Although Mitch had wanted to be married within the next few days, she'd convinced him that wasn't long enough to get ready for even the simplest kind of wedding. Not that she was concerned about the outward trappings—becoming Mitch's wife was all that mattered—but there were such formalities as blood tests and the license to be considered.

In the end Mitch had—somewhat reluctantly—agreed to a week's wait, to allow time for whatever arrangements had to be made and to wind up unfinished business of his own, such as his upcoming trip to Montana to meet with some cattle buyers. The day after his return, the ceremony would take place at the Double C, with just Farley and Homer, Ralph Hubbard, Cloris, and Mitch's other employees and their families in attendance. Cloris and some of the ranch hands' wives were planning a reception for the newlyweds, and Cloris had announced her intention of making the wedding cake herself. She made it clear that she wouldn't entrust such an important assignment to "just anybody."

Serena was so engrossed in her rosy dreams that she didn't notice, until a high wall of rock rose in solemn splendor in front of her, that the terrain was changing dramatically. The gentle, grass-covered slopes were giving way to rough, rocky ground, and the surrealistic peaks she'd seen in the distance were now directly ahead.

As she reined Penny to a halt and gazed about her in fascination, a flash of movement overhead caught her eye. She glanced up to see a bird sharply outlined against the sky. Its wings were backward crescents, and as it soared gracefully, the sun occasionally caught its underside, revealing a creamy white chest barred with black. Serena could sense the restrained power in the broad-shouldered, streamlined body. She watched until it wheeled and disappeared behind a peak, dipping slightly as if to signify that the performance was over.

Once the bird was out of sight, she turned her attention back to the granite peaks that loomed ahead like ancient castles and fortresses. Deep fissures ran vertically down the cliff faces, and horizontal cracks formed wide ledges. The slanting rays of morning sun moved across the towering crags, softening the stark shadows.

The area was so remote that Serena felt as if she must be the first person who had ever set foot here. She knew, of course, that she was being fanciful. As proof that others had been here before her, the fence came all the way up to where the crags jutted up out of the ground and picked up again on the other side—apparently the boundary line was bisected by the rocky formation.

Besides, there were scars cut into the cliff walls, indications that some sort of excavating had gone on here at one time. She also noticed broken, bleached-out bits of timber. The shallow trench that meandered down from the higher ground looked as if it might have once been a creek. Probably water still flowed through it during the rainy season. But now the pebbles and stones that littered its bed were dry and dust-covered.

*Why, this must be the site of that old placer mine,* Serena realized. Clarence Hicks, who owned the rock shop in Cougar Bluff, had said it was on what was now the boundary between her ranch and the Diamond

T. Those pieces of wood were probably all that remained of sluice boxes or rockers.

Max, who had been investigating interesting scents, came bounding back to join her as she dismounted. "C'mon, boy," she said, giving him a pat. "Let's go exploring."

Leaving Penny ground-tied to munch what little grass was left nearby, she spent the next half hour climbing over odd-shaped boulders and peering into cavelike indentations.

As she was finishing her exploration, she noticed that a dark cloud had appeared, seemingly out of nowhere, to block out the sun. She was just starting to wonder if she ought to look around for suitable shelter when a flash of lightning, followed by a low, menacing rumble convinced her that might be a wise move. She located a wide overhanging ledge and ducked under it just as the first drops of moisture fell.

With the next clap of thunder Max rushed to join her. His presence was comforting, and they sat side by side, watching the water making little rivulets in the thirsty ground. She felt a little guilty about leaving Penny out in the rain, but the mare seemed oblivious to the elements as she munched contentedly.

The shower stopped as suddenly as it had started. When Serena and Max emerged from their shelter, the air was warm again. The dark cloud, relieved of its burden, had broken up into wisps of white, each one edged in gold as it reflected the sun's brilliance.

The newly washed pebbles in the creek bed glittered and sparkled. Wouldn't it be exciting if she found a nugget? Serena thought. Although she realized how unlikely that possibility was, she couldn't resist bending down to poke around in the rubble.

As she sifted the rocks through her fingers, she came upon an irregularly shaped clod of—*something*—that looked like dirty white wax. She glanced at it curiously and was about to toss it aside, but when she turned it over, she noticed a bit of blue showing through the grayish-white exterior. With the dust washed away by the rain, the blue material revealed a glossy sheen when the sunlight touched it.

Not a gold nugget, by any stretch of the imagination. Still, it was interesting enough to warrant further investigation. She would ask Mitch if he knew what it was.

Further exploration produced nothing else unusual. Besides, she'd been gone long enough. It was time she started back, before someone got worried and organized another search party.

It was several days before Serena thought about the unusual rock again. When she and Mitch were together, they had more interesting matters than rocks to discuss. And then, all too soon, it was time for him to leave for Montana. Although Serena dreaded being separated from him for even three days, she reminded herself that the sooner he left, the sooner he would get back—and the sooner they could be married.

She was planning to spend the intervening time tying up whatever loose ends remained. She'd already made one trip into Cougar Bluff to choose her wedding outfit, an ankle-length white dress in a quaint, old-fashioned style in keeping with the simple ceremony that was planned. She just needed to find a few accessories to go with it.

As she was getting ready to go into town, she noticed the odd rock, still on her dresser where she had left it. She'd take it with her and ask her friend Clarence if he knew what it was, she decided, dropping it into her shirt pocket.

''Well, if it isn't my favorite customer,'' Clarence said gallantly as Serena entered The Rockhound. ''You're looking mighty perky today. Glad to see you're all recovered from your night out on the range. And I hear there's a wedding coming up. I wish you all the happiness in the world.''

News certainly *did* travel fast around here, Serena thought. She appreciated Clarence's good wishes. She'd been to his shop several times since that first visit, and by now they were fast friends. She'd brought her pendant in, and he'd verified that it was a star sapphire.

''There's no doubt the stone came from somewhere near here,'' he'd told her. ''That particular shade of blue is unique to this area.''

Serena had been touched to think of her father having a stone, possibly from his own ranch, cut, polished, and made into a pendant for his new bride.

''Now, then, what can I do for you today?'' Clarence asked.

She fished the rock from her pocket. ''I have something here I'd like you to look at. Maybe you can tell me what it is. I thought it was kind of interesting."

But when she put it on the counter for Clarence's examination, she was a little embarrassed. The blue showing through, which had given forth such a luster when wet, now had no more sheen than a piece of dull glass. And the outer material—she had learned from the book she'd bought that it was known as the *matrix*—was neither interesting nor unusual. The rock sat there on the counter like a lump of dirty dough.

Clarence seemed to find it worthy of his attention, however. He picked it up and hefted it in his hand, frowning as if he were deep in thought. Then he excused himself and stepped into the back room of his shop, and Serena heard water running. When he returned, the rock was wet. He held it up to the window, turning it this way and that so it could catch the sun. Finally he inspected it minutely with a jeweler's magnifying glass.

Surely he was just humoring her, Serena thought. By now she was feeling a little silly to be taking up so much of his time. "Well, what's the verdict?" she asked at last. "Is it an especially fine example of plain old garden-variety rock?"

Clarence put the stone back on the counter. "Actually, it's an especially fine example of star sapphire. It's a fairly valuable gem—or it will be once it's properly cut and polished."

"Really? I didn't dream it was worth anything. I just picked it up because it was—kind of unusual."

She could hardly wait to tell Mitch about her exciting find.

"Where'd you find it?" Clarence asked. "No—don't tell me. Let me see if I can guess." He picked it up again and studied it, then set it back down. "I'd be willing to bet it came from that old placer mine out on your boundary line."

Serena's eyes widened in surprise. "How did you know that?"

Clarence chuckled. "I'm not psychic, if that's what you're thinking. Your fiancé Mitch has found several stones similar to this one out in that spot. 'Course, that was quite a while back, but I just put two and two together."

Serena felt her excitement draining away, to be replaced by a strange uneasiness. Disjointed phrases echoed in her mind. ". . . Mitch . . . found several stones . . . in that spot. . . ."

"You—you're sure the stones Mitch found came from the same place?" she asked, hoping that she'd misunderstood and that his next words would reassure her.

"No doubt about it. Remember I told you all the gems from a certain area around here were a unique shade of blue? This one"—his glance indicated the stone on the counter—"and the ones Mitch brought in are all that same color. It's almost like a brand. That's what makes these particular sapphires especially valuable."

"Oh." The monosyllable came out sounding flat and

dispirited. She picked up the stone and put it back in her pocket. "Thanks for your help."

Although she knew Clarence was puzzled over her sudden mood change, she had to get out of there. She needed to be alone to think over this disturbing bit of information he had inadvertently revealed.

Serena's head was spinning as she drove home. In spite of her determination not to jump to conclusions, there were several facts that couldn't be ignored. There *were* gems to be found on her land. And Mitch had apparently known about them for some time. Why had he never mentioned them to her?

To be fair, she had to admit the subject wasn't one that was likely to come up in casual conversation. One didn't just say, in the middle of a discussion of irrigation methods or livestock management, "Oh, by the way, did you know there are quite valuable star sapphires out by that old placer mine?" And once they'd become engaged—well, they'd had other things on their minds.

On the other hand, if he'd made an offer to buy her property and he knew it contained something valuable, wasn't he obligated, at least morally, to let her know?

She couldn't help remembering how disgruntled he'd been when she'd delayed in accepting his offer because she'd wanted time to look the place over first. Now it occurred to her to wonder just why he'd been in such a hurry. He'd *said* he was concerned over the ranch being mismanaged, but he could have simply been afraid that if she hung around too long, she might find out about this unexpected source of wealth.

Buying an entire ranch just to gain control of some gems *did* seem rather a drastic step, her common sense told her. Still, in this cattle country, land was never a bad investment. And if he happened to know that land contained a hidden source of wealth, he couldn't lose. He could have known about the gems for a long time and had simply been biding his time. Then when her father had died, maybe he'd assumed this was his golden opportunity, that it would be an easy matter to buy the Double C now. After all, the "daughter back East" would probably be relieved to find someone to take it off her hands. But she'd thrown a monkey wrench into his plans by insisting on coming out here to see the place and then by deciding to stay.

But that was utterly ridiculous, she scolded herself. What was wrong with her that she was having such thoughts about Mitch? He wasn't some shady, fast-talking stranger, intent on cheating her out of what was rightfully hers. He was the man who, less than a week ago, had pledged his undying love for her.

Besides, what reason would Mitch have for trying to put anything over on her? After all, he was already fairly wealthy in his own right. But that still didn't explain why he hadn't told her about the stones.

The thought crossed her mind that maybe he wasn't as well-off as appearances would indicate. Against her will, she found herself creating a scenario. What if he'd suffered business setbacks lately or had had unforeseen expenses and was counting on those gems to see him through a financial crisis?

Or could he just be one of those people who aren't

satisfied with what they already have, who have to keep acquiring more and more wealth? Maybe once he'd discovered the gems, he couldn't be content with just the ones on his side of the boundary line. He had to have hers too. She'd heard tales of men who, during the Gold Rush days, were stricken with "gold fever," who were prepared to go to any lengths to obtain those precious yellow nuggets. No doubt there were some who succumbed to the lure of precious gems in the same way.

All the way home Serena argued with herself. Everything in her cried out against believing Mitch had tried to take advantage of her. She *wanted* to trust in his honesty and integrity. Yet she couldn't come up with any plausible reason why he hadn't told her about the gemstones. And that omission, coupled with the way he'd tried to pressure her into selling her ranch, certainly indicated he had deliberately intended to keep the truth from her.

And when she hadn't given in to his demands that she sell to him, he'd tried another approach. He'd pretended to fall in love with her. Her cheeks flamed at the memory of how easily she'd accepted his declaration of love in spite of the stormy relationship they'd had in the past. Why, she'd practically fallen into his arms!

Was it so unthinkable that he was actually prepared to go so far as to marry her in order to gain control of her land and whatever riches it contained? People got married for less valid reasons, she knew. There was no denying there was a strong physical attraction between them—when they weren't busy opposing each other. Even in her present frame of mind, the memory of his kisses sent a little jolt of excitement through her. If she'd never found out about Mitch's deception, she'd probably have been perfectly happy being his wife.

But she *had* found out. Now, as she saw the situation, she had two choices. She could keep this new knowledge to herself, go ahead and marry Mitch and try to forget that he had tried to deceive her. In her heart, though, she wondered how a marriage based on doubt and distrust could survive.

On the other hand, she could confront Mitch, give him an opportunity to explain why he hadn't told her about the gems. But what if he didn't *have* an explanation? What if he simply took her in his arms and kissed away her fears, as if she'd been imagining things? Then she still wouldn't know the truth, and she was right back where she'd started.

Either way she was bound to lose.

And the knowledge left her with a heavy lump of misery deep inside her.

## *Chapter Twelve*

Mitch wouldn't be back until the day after tomorrow. Serena had two days to decide whether to demand an explanation from him or to keep the knowledge that he'd deceived her locked away inside her.

If she *did* confront him and he couldn't offer any reason for not telling her about the gems—what reason *could* there be? she wondered dismally—then what? Could she go ahead and marry him, anyway? The alternative left her feeling cold and empty.

She'd have to sell the ranch and go back to Windham if she decided against marrying Mitch. It would be unthinkable to stay here and take the chance of running into him constantly—especially if he chose to press his case. She'd already found out the effect his very touch could have on her. How could she hope to hold out against him indefinitely?

Yet the thought of leaving sent a wave of abject misery welling up in her. In the brief time she'd been here, all this had come to mean "home" to her—the ranch itself, the people she'd met. And Farley and

Homer were like family. They'd advised her, supported her, helped her over the rough spots.

She hadn't realized how empty certain areas of her life had been, how devoid of close ties after the death of Gram and then her mother. In the back of her mind there had been the awareness that she had a father, and she had vague intentions of sometime getting to know him, but then even that was taken from her. There had been Kelly, of course, and they were closer than many sisters—but Kelly was in Germany now with her new husband and a whole new life opening up before her.

All this went through Serena's mind as she went about her evening chores. She did the work automatically, drawing it out as long as possible in order to give herself something to do. As she fed Penny her ration of oats, she struggled to hold back tears, wondering if she would be saying good-bye to the little mare before long.

She was relieved that Farley and Homer were busy elsewhere. She was afraid that if she encountered either of them, they would be able to tell something was wrong. And if she explained to them why she was so troubled, they would likely try to defend Mitch's actions.

When she finally ran out of chores to do in the barn, she came inside. With a huge lump in her throat, she wandered through the house, touching now-familiar objects.

She came across a small stack of her father's things tucked away on a shelf. During her first days here she'd sorted out certain items to take back with her as keepsakes. Not that she needed much in the way of material items in order to feel close to her father now. Since that time, she'd absorbed enough of his presence to know that she would be inextricably bound to him for the rest of her life.

Still, there were a few of his belongings she'd wanted to keep—some of his books, the photograph album, and his journal. She had a feeling that if she decided to leave, that last item, especially, would be a comfort to her in the months to come. She knew there would be times when the loneliness would close in around her like a thick pall, when she would feel there wasn't one person in the world who cared about her. If she had something of her father's, written in his own hand, she wouldn't feel quite so bereft.

She picked up the thick notebook and thumbed through it. Except for those passages that concerned her, she'd never gotten around to reading the rest of it. This might be just the time, she decided. With the long, empty evening stretching out before her, her father's journal would be just what she needed to keep unwelcome thoughts at bay.

Curling up in a big, comfortable overstuffed chair and tucking her feet up under her, she leafed through the book, scanning the entries at random. There was one that described a spring flood and how the cattle had had to be moved to a higher pasture before the entire herd was lost. Another entry told of her father's struggles to get parts for the old hay baler.

Farley and Homer were mentioned often, of course, as well as her father's neighbor and close friend, Frank

Tanner, who was then owner of the Diamond T. She came across one passage that read, *Frank's brother's boy, Mitch, came to live with him. Poor kid—his parents were killed in a boating accident. . . .*

After that, interspersed among other comments and bits of information, were occasional references to Frank's nephew, such as, *Seems like a nice boy—good head on his shoulders. Really into Indian lore.*

And later, as Mitch reached his teens, *Had Frank's nephew working for me this summer, getting the hay in. For a kid his age, he puts in a good day's work . . . hard to find good part-time help.*

As Mitch grew older, her father wrote that he was turning out to be a *fine young man,* and that he was *doing a man's work* right along with the Diamond T ranch hands.

And eventually, *Last night I went with Frank and his housekeeper, Cloris, to his nephew's high-school graduation.*

In an entry dated the following fall, Serena read that Mitch had gone off to study modern ranching methods. Then, shortly after he finished college and returned to help run the Diamond T, his uncle died. Although her father's account of Frank Tanner's death was written matter-of-factly, Serena sensed, reading between the lines, how saddened he was by the death of his longtime friend.

*Mitch will be taking over the Diamond T, of course,* her father wrote. *He's young to be running such a big spread, but I think he'll do fine.*

It was obvious that a strong bond of friendship was

developing between the two men, Serena noted as Mitch's name turned up with dismaying frequency. All these references to him were bringing back the ache she'd been trying so hard to suppress. She riffled through the book, determinedly skipping over any mention of his name.

But when the words *peregrine falcon* almost leaped off the page at her, she couldn't resist going back to the beginning of that entry, even though the subject generated unwanted memories. In spite of her resolve to put all thoughts of Mitch out of her mind, her thoughts went back to that early-morning conversation when Mitch had shared a very personal moment with her.

*Spotted an unusual bird out near the old placer mine—small, wings curved back in a sort of crescent. Sure was pretty, the way it soared and dived. When I mentioned it to Mitch, he thought it might be a peregrine falcon, although they're pretty rare these days.*

The next entry on the subject was dated a few days later:

*Mitch got a look at that bird and says it's definitely a peregrine. He thinks there might be a female in the area too, because of the show it was putting on. According to Mitch, they nest on high, rocky crags instead of in trees, and that area out by the mine is perfect for their needs. He seems to know quite a bit about them.*

Apparently Mitch had never told Serena's father the story of that vision quest he'd gone on as a young boy. In spite of her present feelings about him, Serena was touched that Mitch had singled her out to share what was obviously a very private part of his life.

The next few entries also concerned the falcon. A second one, a female, had been sighted, and her father reported that Mitch was keeping as close a watch on the pair as he could without disturbing them.

After that there were almost daily reports on the courtship, with frequent quotes from Mitch. *Mitch is hoping they'll nest out there . . . says one healthy breeding pair could go a long way toward increasing the peregrine falcon population.*

Serena sensed that Mitch's enthusiasm was catching. Her father sounded as if he were becoming as involved as Mitch in the fate of this particular bird. She wondered if the bird she'd sighted might be the falcon he was writing about, or maybe one of its offspring. The thought made her feel very close to her father.

Then, with no warning, came the shattering news: *Found the falcon dead this morning when I was out clearing water holes. It had been shot.*

A shock wave ran through Serena as she read the stark statement. Her father's next words echoed her own feelings. *Sometimes I don't understand what gets into folks.*

After that there was no mention of peregrine falcons for quite a few pages, only a long stretch of brief notations about everyday matters, as if her father was so disheartened over the things some people do that he wanted to put the entire episode out of his mind.

The next time Serena glanced up, she was surprised to notice the dark shadows in the corners. She'd become so engrossed in the journal that she hadn't realized she'd been reading for over an hour. The words were beginning to blur together. She decided to put the journal aside for now.

But as she was about to close it, she came across an entry dated a full two years after the falcon had been killed.

*Mitch told me he spotted a peregrine! Same place as before. This time we're not taking any chances.*

What did that mean, she wondered. *We're not taking any chances. . . .*

Subsequent entries recorded the bird's progress. He was making advances toward a female . . . they were nesting on one of the cliffs . . . and then, when two eggs hatched, *We did it—we have a breeding pair! I feel like a grandfather!*

Serena was up early the next morning, after a night of tossing and turning and vague, restless dreams about star sapphires and abandoned gold mines. She still hadn't made up her mind whether to confront Mitch or to simply keep her knowledge to herself.

She had just finished dressing when there was a knock at the front door. *That's funny,* she thought as she went to open it. Farley and Homer always came to the back door.

But instead of either of the ranch hands, she found

Mitch standing on her front porch. Everything about him—his crisp, dark hair, his jaunty grin, his lithe, sinewy build—exuded a magnetism that almost overwhelmed her. In contrast to her own troubled mood, he radiated vitality and good spirits.

When she was alone, it was easy to convince herself that she could confront him in a mature, unemotional manner. But with him standing so close that she could feel the warmth of his body, she wasn't so sure. Just being near him was enough to make her entire body tingle with awareness and send all her good intentions flying out the window.

He raised an eyebrow, and one corner of his mouth quirked in a smile. "Aren't you going to invite me in?"

Wordlessly she moved out of the way to allow him to enter.

"You don't seem very glad to see me," he observed, stepping inside.

"It's just that I—I wasn't expecting you back until tomorrow."

"I wound up my business early," he explained. "I didn't want to be away from you any longer than I had to. I couldn't keep my mind on cattle—all I could think about was how much I missed you. Those Montana cattlemen must have thought I was addleheaded."

Although his tone was light, there was no mistaking the love in his eyes. With a gentle strength, he swept her into his arms. As he drew her up against him and his lips took possession of hers, she reacted with a traitorous longing that she was powerless to prevent.

By the time they finally drew apart, her limbs felt weak, as if they could barely support her.

This would be the time to voice her suspicions and demand an explanation, while she still had a vestige of self-control left. It was hard to think clearly, however, with Mitch's arms still around her and his fingers tracing soft, enticing patterns up and down her spine.

"I wish we could be married right away," he murmured against her hair. "Even two days is too long to wait."

His words brought her sharply back to reality. Summoning all her willpower, she twisted out of his embrace. Instinctively he reached for her, but she backed away.

"There's something we have to talk about," she blurted out.

He looked down at her, his brows drawing together in a slight frown. "Hey, this sounds serious," he said in a low voice. "Go ahead—I'm listening."

She knew she'd never be able to speak her piece unless she put a little distance between them. She went over to stand by the window.

"When I was out riding a few days ago, I found this unusual rock out by that old placer mine."

"The placer mine!" he exclaimed. "You shouldn't be going out to a remote area like that alone. You could get lost again—"

She waved aside his concern. "When I took the rock into town and showed it to Clarence Hicks, he told me it was a star sapphire and that you'd found several stones like it in that same area. I—I couldn't help wondering why you'd never told me there were valuable stones out there. . . ." Her voice trailed off as she waited for him to draw his own conclusions.

"There wasn't anything to tell. There aren't enough stones left out there to shake a stick at these days." He stared at her in disbelief as her meaning sank in. "Wait a minute, Serena, you don't honestly think I purposely kept them a secret from you!"

"I—I'm not sure what to think. All I'm sure of right now is that you were aware of those stones and you didn't say a word to me about them."

Mitch shoved his hands into his pockets and hunched his shoulders, his features setting into an expression of resignation. *Aha,* Serena thought. *Now the truth comes out.* Funny, though, he didn't have the guilty look of a man who had a confession to make. Sheepish might be a better word—rather like a kid who'd been caught with his hand in the cookie jar. Obviously he didn't consider dishonesty and deception to be very serious offenses.

"Remember when I told you about going on my vision quest and seeing the falcon?"

"Yes," Serena replied, wondering what that could possibly have to do with the matter at hand. She managed to keep her tone impersonal, although the memory of that morning and the personal experience he'd shared with her still gave her a warm feeling inside.

"I know I tried to give the impression that I didn't take the whole incident too seriously. Well, I wasn't being completely honest. I guess those Native American ancestors of mine played a bigger part in shaping my personality than I like to admit. Not that I'm ashamed of my heritage or anything like that,'' he hastened to assure her. ''It's just that believing in vision quests and spirit guides seems a little superstitious these days.'' He paused, and for a second or two that hand-in-the-cookie-jar expression played across his features again.

Serena was caught off guard. She'd expected him to try to sweet-talk her, to brush aside her doubts as if they didn't exist. Instead, he was going on about peregrine falcons and his Native American heritage. Was this some sort of diversionary tactic?

''The truth is,'' Mitch continued, somewhat self-consciously, ''I've always sort of felt a real closeness to the peregrine falcon—almost as if it were my good-luck charm. That's not something I go bandying about, but—well, there it is.''

In spite of her suspicions, Serena felt a pang of tenderness as she sensed how difficult it must be for a proud man like Mitch to admit to what some people might consider a weakness. She brushed the thought aside, however. He was trying to cloud the issue. ''What do peregrine falcons have to do with those gemstones that you neglected to tell me about?'' she asked coldly.

''Oh. I guess I didn't explain about that. You see, the only place those stones were ever found is out by the old placer mine—which has become a nesting area for peregrine falcons. Maybe it's foolish and impractical to overlook what could be a source of income—assuming there were enough sapphires out there to even bother with—but with those falcons so close to becoming extinct, I feel an obligation to protect their nesting grounds. We—your dad and I—were keeping our eyes on a pair out there that was getting ready to nest.''

That fit in with what she'd read in her father's journal, Serena thought. *Mitch is hoping they'll nest . . . one healthy breeding pair could go a long way toward increasing the peregrine falcon population.*

An expression of sadness darkened Mitch's features. ''Somebody shot the male bird. We both suspected it was someone who was out in that area hunting for gems—illegally, of course, since it's private property. There were indications that some digging had gone on in the dry creek bed. There used to be a lot of those stones out there, before the area was picked dry, and they were in demand because of their particular color. Every so often somebody gets wind of them and goes treasure-hunting. Some people think they can get rich quick, and they don't care how much damage they do in the process. The next time your dad and I spotted a peregrine out there, we decided the less said about the stones, the better.''

So that was what her father had meant when he'd written, *We're not taking any chances.* Of course. It was all so clear now. ''Then it—it was because of the peregrines that you kept quiet about the stones.''

Mitch nodded. ''We figured the rumor that there were valuable stones in that area would die a natural death eventually, and then the birds could nest without being disturbed. Not that I'd have kept it from you, of course,'' he said, looking down at her with tenderness. ''Honey, if there'd been anything to tell you, I would have, but there just wasn't anything worth mentioning. . . .''

His voice trailed off, as if a new thought had just occurred to him. ''You thought I purposely kept you from knowing, because I wanted the stones for myself.'' It was a statement, not a question.

Serena winced under the sudden coldness of his gaze.

''If you believed that,'' he went on, ''you must also have believed the reason I want to marry you is to gain control of—of those riches you thought were on your land.'' His voice was flat and impassive. ''You had me tried and convicted before I even had a chance to defend myself.''

Everything he said was true, Serena had to admit. She *had* been convinced there was nothing he could say that would lessen his guilt.

He looked more hurt than angry. ''I thought you loved me. I guess I was wrong, though, if you really believed I could deceive you that way.'' He put his hand on the doorknob.

Serena's heart sank. *It's over now,* a little voice whispered. *You've lost him now with your mistrust and your suspicions.* She might just as well go ahead and have Ralph draw up the papers to let Mitch buy the Double C. She couldn't bear the thought of staying here now.

As he turned to leave, something twisted inside Serena. *Say something,* her heart cried out. *Don't let it end this way*. But she couldn't seem to make her voice obey. The kind of love most people only dream of was about to walk out of her life, while she stood there mute.

"Mitch . . ." she managed to get out, in a thin, trembly voice.

He hesitated, and Serena hardly dared to breathe. Several heartbeats of time stretched into an eternity before he turned back to face her. Nothing in his expression or manner gave any indication of what he was thinking.

"I guess I have to admit you don't have any monopoly on misjudging people," he finally said when Serena thought she could stand the suspense no longer. "When it comes to jumping to wrong conclusions, I'm probably a couple up on you."

"Wh-what do you mean?" she mumbled through lips that felt numb.

"Maybe if I hadn't been so judgmental to begin with, you wouldn't have been so quick to believe the worst about me. When you first came here, I'd already made up my mind that the only reason you wouldn't sell out to me right away was that you were waiting for a better offer—remember?"

"Yes, but—"

"And I'd decided, without hearing your side of it, that it was your fault you'd never had any contact with your father. And later, when I found out you were planning to stay here and work the ranch yourself, I was convinced you were just a spoiled city girl playing games. Boy, I really blew it on that one!" He shook his head. "I knew how mistaken I'd been after I saw you half killing yourself to make a go of the place, but I was too stubborn to admit I'd been wrong. It seems that I've got a few apologies of my own to make."

"What are you trying to tell me, Mitch?" Serena asked softly, hardly daring to hope.

"I guess what I'm saying, in my bumbling way, is that we've both made mistakes. Maybe what we'd better do is wipe the slate clean and start over again from square one."

Serena could almost hear the beating of her heart as she waited for him to go on.

"Do you—do you suppose we could put the past behind us and make a new start?" he continued. "If—if it's not too late?"

A well of happiness bubbled up inside her. "It's not too late," she said softly.

He closed the distance between them in a few long strides. At first he didn't touch her. He simply stood looking down at her, searching her features. Then he put a lean, calloused finger under her chin and, with infinite gentleness, tilted her face up to his.

Then his arms were around her, and he was whispering her name in a voice ragged with emotion. As his lips came down on hers to seal the bond between them, Serena knew that bond would never again be broken.